The Healer aι

Bekah Clark

Cover art by:

Daniela Owergoor: http://dani-owergoor.deviantart.com/

ISBN-13:
978-1721831784

ISBN-10:
1721831789

Chapter One

The winds whipped around me, causing a few loose strands of my flame-red hair to cut across my eyes as I made my way up the trail I had taken so many times before. It was not so much a trail as a small worn path up the mountain that existed because I traveled it so often, just as my mother had before me. This particular slope was the only one that grew telgan root. Telgan root was good for a digestive, and I liked to have it on hand for Old Widow Mae. A short laugh slipped out of me as I thought of the unappreciative grunt she'd give me when she got the digestive next. Not that she was any different from the rest of the village folk. My laugh stopped and I gave a little huff of frustration.

My mother had been the previous healer and her mother had been before her. My great-grandmother had moved to this village from far away. War had driven her search for somewhere peaceful. I couldn't blame her. The drive to heal those gravely injured was powerful, and the consequence of too many healings was a danger. Living in a land during war must have been difficult, at best. The need to heal must have been agony.

I paused and took a deep breath as I let my eyes roam over this particular part of the mountain. My heart swelled at the beauty of it, with the swirling wildflowers of yellow, red, blue, and white dancing in the rough winds that always churned around Mount Caden. The air up here was cool, sweet, and clean. Whenever I arrived on this strip of land, I would always feel both free and at peace. But that freedom and peace did not quell the surge of loneliness in my heart.

Purposefully striding further into the clearing, I turned to gaze down at my village home. Nestled between two rivers, Vella's red walls and roofs were a stark contrast to the rich greens of the area. The people believed the color red protected them from the various so-called monsters and demons that dwelled in the mountains. If there were such things, they never once came out and bothered me. And though I would never say it to anyone, I very much doubted the deep red would save them.

A sardonic laugh slipped out of my lips as I thought of the last time I had been called to heal someone. When I arrived, I could see that everyone in the house wore dark red except the patient, who stared up at me with wide, fearful eyes of blue. When his gaze met my jade eyes, he had trembled violently as dread took over his face. In the village, people only had brown or blue eyes. The green ran exclusively in my family, a so-called sign of our witch heritage. And then, of course, there was the flame red of my hair. When I was little, the other children would tease me by claiming that my true father was a demon and not the honorable Constable Jorn. When I'd looked into that young man's eyes, I realized people still thought that.

Despite what I knew of their story, how my mother managed to get my father to marry her in this village of fools eluded me. At twenty-two, marriage was no longer option for me. Girls in my village were all married before they turned nineteen. I had come to accept that my family line would end with me. Even though I was sure there were a couple of men in the village whom I could tempt for a night or two, I would not add being fatherless to the list of crimes any child of mine would carry. Besides, the thought of sharing my bed with a man who thought of me as a demon's offspring was unappealing.

Shaking my head to clear my mind, I turned back to my task. The mountainside was full of numerous plants, so I toiled meticulously as I gathered telgan roots, fae flowers, and various other herbs and wild fruits that I used in the many items I sold as the town's herbalist. Because of my heritage, they denied me the lofty term *apothecary*. It didn't matter because everyone knew my goods were the best. And those items were how I made the money I needed to survive. True healings I did for free. I felt compelled to save lives when I could feel their pain. The items I made as an herbalist complemented my healings as well as provided several beauty aids.

I labored for a few hours before I started to make my way down the mountain and across the small footbridge to the red walls of my village. Just inside the gates, I nodded to Constable Kean. He was my uncle, my father's brother. His gruff nod in reply showed he still had not warmed to me. My father had been away from the village when his horse threw him and he died. Kean blamed it on his association with my mother. A few months later, my mother, Aren, took her own life out of grief. She did it while I was gathering herbs a few miles away and was long dead by the time I returned home. Even my gifts could not bring back the dead.

Although I couldn't understand such a choice, I didn't blame her. How could I? Not when such a rare bond had existed between their two souls. They had been True Mates, and her grief was more intense than she could bear. Even my love wasn't enough to replace the loss of my father. A sigh escaped my lips. If my True Mate existed, he was not in this village. I would have known by now. Even though it would be difficult to come together, I often let myself believe that if we could have, I would be happy—and not so alone.

Letting out a sharp breath, I shook my head. None of that wallowing, I warned myself, that path leads to madness. I had my work and it was fulfilling. Just the other week, I'd fixed little Eesa's ankle. People bought my teas, potions, lotions, and creams, and even if they were not grateful, they were happy with the results. It was a simple life of genuinely helping people.

After entering my warm little home, I took a deep, calming breath and walked to the table where I worked. Sorting out the multitude of plants, I separated them by kind before I began to prepare them. Singing to myself, I secured the herbs I wanted to dry into little bundles to hang. Those I needed to use fresh, I placed in the various baskets I had. I jumped at a sudden, loud banging on my door. "Come in," I called out. It was unusual for someone to come in the front door, and my heart skipped a beat in worry.

Lidia, the finest seamstress in the village, entered in a rush. "Zianya! It's Kiara. She just gave birth before her time. The baby is fine, but she won't stop bleeding!"

Heart thundering with worry for the young, new mother, I dashed out the door and down the lane. Kiara lived several blocks down, and I put a rush into my legs, wanting to make it in time. When I burst into the house, I could hear the healthy wail of a newborn, but I could feel the dark coils of impending death. I dashed into the room, where the dark-haired midwife glared at me. Senna had never liked me because she thought I took business from her. I didn't understand why because I never assisted in births. "There's nothing to be done," Senna said gravely. "You may as well leave, girl."

As long as I'd known her, Senna never said my name. I growled at her, "For shame. You know that I can save her."

Senna spat at me, "She doesn't need a witch. She needs to die with her soul intact!"

My need to touch Kiara and heal her was overwhelming, but I fought it, and that fight caused a little stab of pain to run through me. No matter how much I wanted to heal Kiara, I couldn't do such a thing if her mother would not let me. Fortunately, Senna was not her mother.

Turning my eyes to the wide ones of Jeen, I pressed, "I can save your daughter. Do you want your grandchild growing up without her because of foolish superstition spouted by an old woman whose biggest problem with me is that she thinks I take her business? I am not a witch. I'm a healer. You grew up with my mother — was she evil?"

Jeen met my eyes and then she nodded grimly. "Stand aside, Senna. Zianya can save my daughter."

"But she's—"

"Stand aside!"

As Senna walked by, her deep blue eyes pierced me as she snarled, "I still say you're a witch."

I brushed by her without another look and sat beside Kiara. My fingers tenderly stroked back her lovely blonde locks. I made soft, comforting sounds as I let my power sink into her and take her pain from her. She relaxed, and everyone in the room took a breath. Kiara opened her brown eyes and looked at me with a fearful gaze. Putting reassurance into a gentle smile, I stroked her hair again. She relaxed further, and I let the warmth of my healing spread down into her abdomen where the bleeding just didn't want to cease. Pieces of me slipped away, weakening my body as they wove into her and knit together all the areas where she bled. I trembled as the energy left me. Finally, I relaxed. Her body was well, and I knew she would live. Leaning back, my eyes ran over Kiara, who was softly sleeping. Sweat sprung out on my forehead as I pushed back my own need to collapse. I raised my eyes to her mother.

"Let her rest. She'll need plenty of that, and water. Her blood needs to rebuild, but she will live. Come by the shop in the morning and I'll get you a tea that will help promote new blood. If she takes it, she should not nurse the child for at least a full day after she consumes it. Perhaps a wet nurse could be used during that time. I do recommend she take it because her recovery will be much improved."

"You just want to sell your wares," Senna hissed. Ignoring her, I braced myself for the weakness that was bound to take me, and rose. Despite that, a shiver coursed through me. Time was slipping away, and there wasn't much of it before I wouldn't be able to stand.

"She'll heal either way, but she'll be stronger faster if she takes the tea."

Jeen shook her head. "She won't need it."

That would have been it, but I'd seen that expression in people's eyes before. Now she was saying she wouldn't come—but she would. Schooling my face into one of neutrality, I gave a quick nod and made my way toward the door. A quiver ran through me, and I faltered before catching myself on the doorframe because I knew no one else would. They all knew a healing took it out of me. One time after a healing, I collapsed in the street. Everyone knew where my home was, everyone knew my door was always open. No one helped me back to my home. They left me there to wake in the morning, freezing and dirty. I'd had to drink a lot of cold-soothe tea after that.

Stumbling along down the road, I wished Kiara lived closer to me. The toll was chasing me, and I wanted to make it back to my home before it took me. As I made my way, I wished the other midwife, Xel, had been there. The younger woman was more open-minded about my healing. I collapsed just outside my door. Fighting the urge to just rest in the street again, I pushed myself to rise and make my way into my home. Once inside, I stumbled along to the patients' room on the first floor. My loft bedroom was too difficult for me to get to at this point. Crumpling onto the bed, sweet oblivion took me.

That night I dreamed of a man with emerald eyes. He was tall, powerful—and even though I saw his eyes, I could not make out his face. I felt drawn to him and didn't understand why. As I was about to ask him who he was in the dream, I awoke to the sound of banging on the back door. A deep groan escaped my lips as I tried to focus on waking up. With great effort, I rose and made my way out of the room and around the large, old farm table that was cluttered with most of my herbs. Opening the large, red-painted oak door, I was not surprised to find Jeen standing there in a red cloak, hood low, glancing around to make sure no one saw her.

I smiled. "Come in."

She looked me over with critical eyes.

I meekly said, "Sorry about my appearance. A healing takes it out of me." My stomach took that opportunity to grumble loudly. Heat filled my cheeks as I made my way to the boxes of teas I had prepared just last week. There were certain preparations I always kept on hand, and this tea for Kiara was one of them. Grabbing a large, blue glass jar, I filled it with some tea from the box and then I went back over to Jeen.

"Ten, please."

"Ten anstals? Really?" She frowned at me. Some people thought that because I healed for free, my herbs should be free or, at least, very cheap.

"I'm sorry, but it's a lot of work to get those particular leaves and prepare them properly. This will help her recover faster." If I didn't hold to my price, word would get out and soon everyone would demand cheaper prices. I couldn't afford to live like that. Besides, she knew my goods worked. Jeen had come to me a few years ago when Kiara's face had broken out with acne. She was trying to marry off her daughter, and she didn't want to ruin her chances for a good match. My salve had her cleared up in less than a week. Since then, Kiara always bought creams and potions from me. Jeen was a little less willing. But she knew it would work.

Grumbling, she handed me the money and took the tea. She opened the door, eyes darting around as she yanked her hood lower on her head, and stole out, moving quickly down the back alley.

Shaking my head, I closed the door and made my way into the kitchen. From the icebox, I pulled out some cold chicken from the night before. Starvation won over my desire to make a sandwich, and I devoured the entire remaining chicken straight from the container. Post healings, two things occurred: a deep need for sleep and then a deep need for food. If I didn't have both, I feared what would happen to me. Once the chicken was gone, I found myself still hungry, so I checked my large iron woodstove — which was still warm from the remaining coals — and added some fuel to it. I put a cast iron pan on the cooktop and grabbed my bread. I made it myself with wild wheat, seeds, and herbs. Cutting into it, I covered one side thick in butter and set two slices into the pan. Then, I got a kettle going so that I could make some teilen tea, a restorative.

Once I was full and feeling like my usual self, I cleaned the kitchen and then washed up. Dressing in my gray cotton skirt and plain white shirt, I got to work once again on separating the herbs. The day went by as it normally did. Every so often, someone would knock on the back door and buy one of my wares. I silently begged the Spirits that no one would require a healing that day. If someone did come by, I wouldn't be able to resist the need to heal them. I knew if I did, I'd exhaust myself at the very least. Too many healings were just unhealthy for any healer.

When the ninth hour of the day arrived, the bells of the Temple of Caden reverberated through the village and everyone was required to go because it was the fourth day of the week. Letting out a deep groan, I hardened myself as I put my work away. I loathed going to the temple. The people of the village worshipped the Spirit of the mountain, but if he was truly some powerful Spirit, I didn't understand what such a powerful being wanted. Did the Spirit even care about the people of this village? He might have, but his priest was Senna's husband and he often made his sermons about avoiding the snare of witches. He never said me, but I knew that was what he meant. The only people in the village who called me witch to my face were the priest, Colm, and his wife, Senna. Every other person in the village either had experienced a healing or knew someone healed by my mother or me. So even though they feared us and avoided associating with us, they wanted us around to save them.

The temple was the largest building in the village in the center of town and had a triangular layout with the podium taking up one point within. Not only was its roof deep red, but the entire exterior was. The point was that evil could not pass into a building that was red. For that very reason, my great-grandmother had painted our doorways red to prove she was not evil. Sometimes I think those doors saved our family more than once.

Inside the temple, wood beams painted red held up the massive structure. The walls were a bright white, and the pews were a dark red. I sat toward the back in my usual spot. Silently, I watched everyone else as they made their way toward the front. Fear darkened their eyes when they'd cast their gaze on me. It didn't matter because as long as I walked into this temple and sat on these red pews, the priest could not point me out as a witch during a sermon. After all, how did I get into the temple if I were evil?

Colm started droning on. I tried not to listen to him. It was more of the same: stay away from evil, praise the Great Spirit Caden for his protection, and keep the mind and body pure. Today he added the importance of shunning witches, while not naming me specifically. No doubt at Senna's prompting. Such a thing always occurred right after a healing. For a day, my sales would be low, and then people would forget. Good thing most people did their business in the morning, before Colm's sanctimonious discourses.

As I took to my feet, a hush fell over the group and I didn't need to see to feel the eyes of the people who had been talking after the sermon. But I did anyways. I dipped my head with a soft smile and turned away, intent on leaving the temple. There was a red-framed painting of Mount Caden near the door. Letting an air of reverence settle over me, I studied the painting before I placed my hand on the red frame. Behind me, there was a gasp, as if they expected me to burst into flames. When I did not, people started talking once more, and I slowly left the temple. I didn't want to hurry and appear to be fleeing.

Outside, I took a deep breath and headed toward my home. I kept my head high as I made my way down the lane. Inside, emotions boiled and I fought to keep them from my face. This village was all I knew, and it was killing me a little each day. Sometimes I actually had a little understanding of why my mother took her life. Without her True Mate, what was for her here? Only me—and now I was slowly fading away from loneliness. I took a deep breath and tried to shove that feeling away. It didn't work.

When I entered my home, I was sorely tempted to curl in my bed and let grief take me. But I was going to resist. Instead, I made myself a sandwich of cheeses and fruits and put on the kettle for tea. As I ate and drank, I took a mental inventory of what I had collected the day before. Tomorrow I'd have a slow day sales-wise, so I'd focus on replenishing what I sold. When I finished my meal and cleaned up, I pulled out one of my mother's old books and curled up on the couch to read. Her books had been my great-grandmother's, and she had bought them when she had first entered Renth in order to be able to learn our written language. I didn't know the name of her homeland, and I always wondered why she left. Had no part been free of war? I didn't know about that. However, her books brought me on adventures set far away from my small village. I pondered how she could have been so strong to move here all alone. Could I ever make such a change?

As I read, my eyes grew heavy, and I fell asleep on the couch. I dreamed of faraway places and eyes that were an infinite emerald. It was calming, and for once, I slept deeply, even though I had not done a healing.

Chapter Two

The loud commotion outside my door drew my attention. Curious, I dragged open the large, red, oak door to find two men bent low under the weight of a third larger man. His head dangled forward, midnight-black hair obscuring his face. Blood was smeared over the shredded remains of his shirt. Behind them, a crowd of people followed, murmuring to one another. The closer they got, the more my need to heal swept through me. I looked back at the man and realized he was still bleeding profusely. "Quick, bring him in."

Once they were inside, I directed them to the patients' room. My eyes darted along his form as I opened his stained shirt and continued checking him over for wounds. There was a large gash across his chest and several stab wounds. "Who did this to him?"

Lane, who had recently taken over the general store for his father, said in a gruff voice, "I don't know, Zianya, we found him down by the river. He looks almost dead, but . . . well, we thought maybe…"

"I can heal him," I said confidently, the urge to sink my power into him becoming more difficult to resist. "Leave him here and I'll take care of him. Tomorrow, after I'm sure he's well enough, I'll send for Kean and he can question him. Right now, he's too weak for anything."

Lane's eyes slid over me with an expression that sent an unpleasant shiver down my spine. "I can stay, if you want."

Despite my revulsion, I smiled up at him, suppressing the tremor within me and plastering my face with a professional cool. He never made any secret of what he wanted from me. However, what he wanted was fleeting, a one-time thing, and I was not the type of woman who was willing to lay with a man without my heart in it. Besides, I had enough of a reputation in Vella—I didn't need to add to it with reality. "I'm fine, Lane. Honestly, after a healing, I'm so exhausted. And his wound is deep. He'll sleep soundly for a long time after."

Fortunately, Lane and his brother left after that. Chewing my bottom lip, it took me a moment to decide to do something I rarely did: I locked my doors. It wasn't that I didn't trust Lane…no. I wasn't going to fool myself. I didn't trust Lane. Just the other day, I had overheard him talking with some of the other men and it had me worried. I wondered what he was truly capable of since his recent comments had set me on edge.

Returning to my patient, my eyes roamed over him for a long moment, which was unusual for me to do. He was tall, taller than the men of the village were. I probably would have only come up to the middle of his chest. And he was well formed—muscular, with shoulders wider than I had ever seen. It was the body of a warrior, I realized. I'd never met one before. The few constables of our village rarely had anything to do, and they often had a paunch. Not like the flat planes of this man's stomach. Biting my bottom lip, I felt a flutter of heat run through me. Shaking my head, I tried to clear it as shame burned through me. This wasn't like me. This man was a patient. Softly stroking his midnight hair off his face, I tried to get a sense of all his wounds. Instead, I found myself realizing he was ruggedly handsome, which was something that I just never allowed myself to realize about my patients. I growled to myself, "Stop thinking like this."

I focused again. When I finally understood the extent of his injuries, I let my power seep into him. As I did, I found each wound and knit them together. When I was done, I took a deep, shuddery breath. Going to my work area, I grabbed some tea leaves that would strengthen him. I rocked back and forth, trying to stay awake as I brewed the tea. Once it cooled, I slowly let it trickle down his throat. When I was done, I collapsed onto the couch and fell into a deep sleep.

As I awoke, before I opened my eyes, I realized I was swaying gently from side to side. I moaned as my eyes finally fluttered open and darted around. It was then that I noted I was on a horse riding deep in the mountains. It was late in the day, and the air was fresh. The next thing I noticed was an arm around my waist and a warm body at my back. I struggled to get free and off the horse.

"Relax, lass. I'll not harm you." A slightly accented voice that was inviting and rich, like dark honey, spoke in my ear.

"Who-who are you?" I asked, my heart racing wildly and my voice stuttering in fear.

"I'm Torric."

I gathered my courage before I finally glanced up at him. The warrior that I had healed now seemed to be my captor. His eyes were like deep emeralds, and they gazed down at me with a tender smile that softened his striking features. I frowned, which just made his smile widen as amusement twinkled in his eyes. "Don't worry, lass. You're safe with me."

"Safe?" I cried in alarm. "You took me from my home! What do you want?"

"Your services are needed. I can't go back without you."

I blinked and fixed my eyes ahead, trying to find an excuse to be returned to my home. I said, "I'm useless without my herbs and potions and the like."

He laughed. "Look behind you to the right."

Sure enough, there was another horse loaded down with two large and intricately carved dark-stained wooden boxes, which appeared to be my grandmother's. In fact, I knew they were because I'd recognize those flowers anywhere. I sighed and looked forward. A wave of dizziness came over me.

"I need to eat," I said softly.

"You can eat when we stop for the night," he replied absently.

"No, I must eat now," I wearily muttered.

"Lass, you need to wait."

My stomach growled loudly and I trembled, feeling another wave of dizziness take me. I gasped, "You don't understand. After a healing, I have two requirements: rest and food, in that order. Your healing was particularly difficult, and so I've slept a lot later than I normally do, and now that I'm awake, I must eat. Please."

He turned my face to study me, emerald eyes turning thoughtful. Then he smiled. "Very well. But if you try to run, lass, I'll catch you before you get home."

It hit me then that I would have to bide my time. If I were to flee, it would have to be when he did not expect it, not to mention when I was not weak with the need for sustenance. He slowed to a stop and dismounted, and then powerful arms picked me up as if I weighed nothing and set me on the ground. I'd never seen so many muscles on a man's arm before. My knees went weak and I almost collapsed, but he swept me into his arms to steady me. Our eyes met, and something in that look caused a flow of heat to run through my veins and pool low in my belly. The intensity of his gaze filled me with a sense of yearning, and I wondered briefly how different things would have been if he hadn't kidnapped me. Yet, that was the thing—he had.

A wicked light gleamed in his eyes as he smiled, and I turned away. Softly, I said, "I need to sit."

Holding onto my arm, he guided me to an overturned log and sat me down. I waited while he reached into his saddlebag and brought me some bread and cheese. I tore into it hungrily. I could feel him watching me as I ate.

Glancing up at him, I spoke in a low tone, "I'll need more. After a healing as big as yours, I'll need a lot more than this. I most definitely need meat."

He frowned. "Why is that?"

I had never shared this with anyone and I wondered if I should with him. However, he needed to know. Obviously, since he had packed up my medicines, he needed me to be his healer. He said he would not harm me, and for reasons I didn't understand, I trusted that to be true. The trouble was, people seemed to think I was a never-ending supply of healing power.

Exhaling softly, I came to a decision. "When I heal, I give some of myself to my patient. There are limits to what I can do. If you had been any closer to death, I would not have been able to heal you for fear of my own death. Although it would have been extremely hard for me to ignore the need to heal you, I would have also felt a need not to touch you. I know that's confusing, but that's probably the best explanation. When I perform a healing, I need a lot of rest, and then I need to eat. A lot. If I don't eat enough food, my body consumes itself, and I lose weight. If that happens too many times, I can die. Because of that, between healings, I consume a lot of food, which is why I'm not as thin as the village girls."

He grinned at me. "Lass, you're small with the kind of curves a man wants on his woman. I'd not complain about that."

Rolling my eyes, I tore another chunk of bread off and chewed. As I ate the seed bread, I let my eyes roam the area. We had traveled far, with no landmarks I recognized; I was actually unsure of where we were. He must have left in the night and rode hard. Deep down, I wondered if anyone in Vella would miss me. I snorted. Probably only when they needed a healing, and no doubt they'd curse me for not being there.

"I'm serious about needing more food." I met his emerald eyes with a level gaze. He stared at me long and hard. Then he nodded and headed into the woods. "Where are you going?"

He called back, "To look for small game."

Sitting there, I nibbled on some cheese and contemplated the idea of running while he was gone. The trouble was, I was lost. The other truth was, that I was too in need of meat to get very far. Torric had been on the borderline of my abilities. For now, I would stay with him. If we passed any villages, I'd take a horse in the night and go.

After I finished what food he left me, I felt drowsy again. Closing my eyes, I let myself drift. I knew I should be afraid of what was to come, but I wasn't. Torric may have elicited a reaction out of me, but it was not one of fear. Lane's gaze may have caused my blood to run cold with the idea he'd take what wasn't his — but not Torric. His emerald eyes danced with the promise of passion, but only if I wanted it.

I would not want it, I told myself. Shaking my head, I reminded myself that he had taken me from my home.

Some time during this inner debate, sleep took me. I awoke to the smell of meat and the crackling of the fire. Opening my eyes, I found Torric on the other side of the fire, a bird on a spit above it. His fiery gaze was on me, and my blood boiled. I closed my eyes again and doused that flame with the reminder that he stole me. Once again, I opened my eyes, and then I sat up and stretched.

Even at this distance, I could tell his eyes were lazily perusing my body. "You shouldn't have slept like that, lass. Anyone could have taken you."

I let out a short laugh. "Someone already did. You know, my powers have limits, and healing you took a lot out of me — as I said."

He grew thoughtful. "How limited?"

I let my eyes fall to the cooking bird and carefully considered how much I would tell him. I needed to make sure he didn't think he could use me as a healer on a battlefield. "One healing per day. And if the injuries are too grave, I have to wait several days to get back my strength. That's why I fell asleep. Also, if I heal people too many days in a row, I'll start to lose weight and grow weak, which can cause me to die. Fortunately, at home, I don't usually have more than one healing every so often."

He frowned as he took in that information. Then he asked, "Why do you think of that place as home? Beautiful lass like you…and not one of those village boys has married you yet?"

My cheeks ignited and indignation caused my voice to rise. "Why are you assuming I'm unmarried?"

He frowned, his face twisting as if he didn't like the idea that I was. He growled, "Are you?"

I tilted my head and met his eyes with defiance as I retorted, "That's my business."

He smiled knowingly, and a flash of irritation filled me. Smugly, he replied, "There were no signs of a husband in your home. Besides, on my way here, I encountered many people around here who took one look at my green eyes and they backed away in fear. I heard them speak of the red-haired witch of Vella, and they wondered why they tolerated her."

"I'm not a witch!"

His laugh was vibrant and warm. Surprise coursed through me when it soothed me. "Aye, I know that, lass. They're superstitious fools."

Smirking, I glanced away. "That, they are. They used to tease me and tell me that a demon was my real father. They think red protects them from evil, but I guess my hair is too much like the color of fire for them to accept that. You wouldn't mind, my mother, grandmother, and great-grandmother all had red hair. My family has been healers in Vella for a long time. Since my great-grandmother came to the village. And yet, they still look at us as evil. They come in the back door for potions and teas and creams, and yet…"

My roughening voice trailed off, and I fought the tears that were threatening to fall. Closing my eyes, I took a deep breath to brace myself.

Suddenly, a solid body was at my side and a warm arm went around my shoulders. Hauling me into his massive chest, Torric's fingers wove through my hair in gentle caresses until I calmed. In spite of that calming, his embrace sparked a flip-flop in my heart.

"Where I'm from, lass, flame-red hair is considered a blessing and a mark of beauty. Our healers all have such hair. Or they did."

"What do you mean *did*?"

Turning to him, I found his eyes on me. They were soft pools of emerald that promised tenderness and shelter. He smiled sadly. "Great war ravages our lands. It's what keeps your homes safe— we border between you and the darkness of the West. Once, there were many healers. Then, in the time of my great-grandfather, assassins from the West came with one purpose: to kill any who possessed the gift of healing. So they targeted those with red hair. Some of our healers scattered. I think you're descended from one of them. What I hope is that you'll help my king."

He scowled and focused his eyes on the dancing blaze of the campfire. His voice grew low and grave as the light of the flames competed with the light of the cloudy day on his face. "My king was poisoned, and he's wasting away. Four warriors were sent East in hopes of finding a healer. On the road, nine bandits attacked me. Three shot me in the back with arrows before they descended. They took all I had and left me for dead."

Bandits had been a problem for some time in our area. That was why I stuck to my own paths. As his words sunk in, my eyes slipped over to the sword on his back, the bow lying not far from me, the quiver of arrows beside it, and then back to him, questioningly. He grinned. "Before we left, I made a trip to your armory. Hopefully, no one will mind."

I laughed. My uncle would be furious. Then I almost cried. He'd be furious about the weapons, but not about me. I took in a shaky breath, and Torric once again crushed me against his chest. "There, there, lass. I promise I'll keep you safe."

"That's not it. I was just thinking how the only time any of them will miss me is if they broke a leg or something."

He turned my face so my eyes met his and he grinned broadly. "Back at my home, you'll be honored, revered. Never you worry, lass."

"So says my kidnapper."

He laughed heartily, releasing me to turn the spit. The fact that I suddenly missed his arm around me struck my heart. He paused and nodded. "This should be done."

Grabbing the spit, he brought the bird over to me. I wondered what it was briefly before I dug into it. It didn't taste particularly good, but I was starving from the healing, so I consumed the dried out meat hastily. I had always found that meats helped me get my strength back better than any other foods. I was halfway done when I raised my eyes to him. Embarrassment flushed my cheeks, and I handed the spit to him. "I'm sorry. You must be hungry, too."

He laughed. "I'm fine, actually. I ate at your home before we left, as well as some of the seed bread I used to lure the bird close."

"So what did you take from my home?"

"Besides all of your food? Every jar of yours that I could pack into those two wooden boxes. I made sure to grab some of everything since I wasn't sure what you'd need. I would've tried to find your money, too, but time was running out. I did grab a book that looked important."

Nodding, I went back to devouring the bird that I suspected was a small, wild game hen. After a time, I said, "When we get to your home, I'll check for what plants I need. What's the name of your home, anyway?"

"The lands are called Glane. My city is Kingshold."

Ice coursed through my veins. My hands trembled as I said, "You're a barbarian of the West? But I thought you said you held back the evil from there!"

He laughed. "Barbarians? So that's why they don't help. Lass, if it wasn't for us barbarians, darkness would sweep across this land."

I finished off my meal and cast the bones into the fire. There was a danger greater than the barbarians? It was hard to comprehend such a thing. But more than that, it was possible I came from those very lands. Or, at least, my great-grandmother did.

My eyes rose to Torric, and I ignored the quickening of my heart. Could I just blindly believe what he said? It was possible he'd say anything to keep me and have me heal his barbarian king. My eyes roved the area where we rested. I couldn't leave now. However, the moment he felt secure that I would not leave, I would make my escape.

"If you're done, we need to get going, lass."

I nodded feebly, feeling numb inside. I didn't want to go west. I didn't want to face whatever darkness lay there. However, Torric put out the fire, gently grabbed my arm to haul me up, and took me to the horse. His strong arms lifted me up and placed me on the saddle before he swung up behind me. He wrapped one arm around my waist and took the reins with the other. With that, we were once again cantering west.

And what hope did I have? No one would come for me. And if I did escape, what about the bandits? If I ran into them on my way home, there was no telling what they'd do to me. I shivered, and he tightened his arm around me. "Cold, lass?" His voice was gentle with concern.

It took everything for me to find my voice. I softly breathed, "Yes." My eyes closed, but all I could feel was the fire of his chest against my back, the warmth of his arm around my waist, and his soft, soothing breath at my temple. It was hard to think that he would hurt me the way I had been taught barbarians would harm us. Was I treating him the way my neighbors treated me? If what he said was true, then my great-grandmother was a barbarian. Plus, there was this great darkness in the West from which, he claimed, his people protected us. I just didn't understand so many things. How was I going to know the right course?

One thing was certain—with each passing moment, I was closer to his home and farther from mine. Each day I would only get more lost. I should have risked running when he went off to get food for me. If I had searched his saddlebags, I may have found more to eat. Instead, I had squandered my chance.

I didn't realize I was weeping until a gentle, calloused hand brushed tears from my cheeks. His arm tightened around me and his lips kissed my temple. I knew he was trying to comfort me, but that just made the tears fall more freely. "Hush now, lass. I promise you'll be safe. And once we're in your new home, you'll be happy."

"Yes," I choked out. "Until an assassin comes to kill me. I won't be safe there. I want to go home!"

His other arm came around me, and he hugged me to him. He whispered in my ear, "I wish I could take this pain from you, lass, but it'll be all right."

"My name is Zianya!"

He chuckled softly. "Once you're with your own people, Zianya, you'll be happy. I promise you."

"But you are taking me from my people!"

He exhaled softly. "I know you can't see it now, lass, but those aren't your people. If they were, they'd accept you."

I stiffened in his arms. "How do you know they don't accept me? You could construe what I said as the rantings of a girl who is feeling bad for herself. Even before I said anything, you asked how I could think of it as home."

He growled and I shook nervously. "Sorry," he said. "I didn't mean to frighten you. But if some man on a horse started to carry off one of the young women of my village, I would've stopped him. Right there, at the gate, your constable looked at you, then me, and then he *stepped aside*. He was unwilling to help you for fear of his own life."

Tears rapidly slipped down my cheeks and I wept freely. My own uncle had abandoned me to this barbarian of the West. He didn't even try to stop him, didn't even worry over my well-being with this warrior. Torric did his best to comfort me, but I was inconsolable as I sobbed in his arms. Eventually, he gave up and just held me tight. Soon after, I exhausted myself and fell into the sweet abyss of sleep.

Chapter Three

The cotton scent of my grandmother's blue-gray quilt surrounded me as consciousness slowly crept into my mind. It was my favorite quilt, with intricate stitches weaving a different plant on each square. I nuzzled into it, remembering when I was little, watching her put in every loving stitch as she explained the process of quilting. When my mind cleared of sleep, I realized I was out under the stars with a roaring fire pouring out waves of heat beside me.

Suddenly, the events of the day came crashing down around me. I let out a groan and burrowed deeper into the quilt, not wanting to face reality. To my right, I heard a honey-warm chuckle. Peeking out, my eyes caressed Torric's powerful form as he was scraping his scruff off with a sharp knife. His shoulder-length midnight hair swirled in the breeze, glinting in the firelight. The men of my village all had beards, especially the older ones who held places of importance in Vella. I wondered if it was different in the West.

As I looked at him, I guessed his age to be close to twenty-eight, though probably a little shy. I wondered if he had a woman waiting for him at home, and that thought sent a jolt of cold water through my veins.

"What's Kingshold like?" I asked softly, as I finally sat up and watched the flames weaving patterns in the night. Every so often, my eyes darted to his hair, his eyes, and his bare chest. I'd never seen a man like him before, with a body honed like carved stone. Every large muscle defined so beautifully, so unlike the slighter frames of the men of Vella.

He flashed me a heartfelt smile before telling me, "The castle is in the center of the city, with a single huge spiral tower in the center. The city itself has a large black wall protecting it."

Curiosity filled me. "Red roofs to keep out evil?"

He laughed. "No, but roofs of various colors. We don't look upon red the way they do here in the East."

My stomach grumbled and I glanced away, hoping he hadn't heard it. His deep chuckle told me it was too late. Heat touched my cheeks as I wished that my stomach wasn't so prone to loud noises.

As I purposefully gazed at the woods, he said, "Hungry? I was waiting to put the meat on for you to wake up. I'll get that going and bring you some bread and butter to tide you over."

He busied himself for a little while, then came over and handed me a couple of buttered slices of bread. My eyes met his and I inhaled quickly. The air had a sudden tinge of cinnamon and a strong, woodsy scent. I realized it was him. Feeling a flush sweep into my cheeks, I whirled my gaze back to the fire. It took a few moments for me to find my voice. "Thank you. Can I ask you something?"

"Of course."

"Are green eyes common in the West?"

When he didn't speak right away, I glanced up to find him watching me. He smiled and put the spit over the fire with a couple of hares on it. Once that was going, he sat next to me. "Very common—about as common as the others. People reacted badly to me but until now, I didn't realize green was that uncommon here, hmm?"

I let out a long breath. "Just another sign that I must be evil." I tried to sound amused by it but failed miserably as the words came out a bit strangled.

He growled, "I could knock those bastards around. Having a healer is a blessing, and they've treated you as a curse."

I let his words sink into me for a moment before I responded. "People fear what they don't understand. It's just how they are. You can't allow yourself to hate them for it."

He shook his head. "Where I'm from, you'd be respected."

Meeting his even gaze, a smile crept across my lips. I wondered what it would have been like, growing up surrounded by appreciation and admiration. Would I still be me? Or would I be arrogant? "Your healers, they must have been rich."

He laughed. "Do you heal for money?"

My lips twisted, wondering what he was getting at. "Well, I sell my wares."

Leaning closer, he grinned down at me. "You sell your wares, but do you heal for money?"

Tilting my head I asked, "How do you know that?"

"While there are no known healers around now, it's a known fact that a healer feels compelled to heal someone who's wounded. It's only when a person is gravely wounded that they can resist. A self-preservation response, I was told."

My eyes narrowed. "You obviously had this information before my explanation the other day. How do you know this?"

"My grandmother was the last known healer in our area. There may be others, but they're in hiding."

There was great sorrow in his eyes, and before I could stop myself, I reached out and gently stroked his face. His eyes turned to mine, emerald pools filled with emotion and sudden desire.

I turned from him, trying to fight my own response as I drew my hand away. "I'm sorry about your grandmother."

Softly, he said, "I was twelve when she died,"

"I was sixteen." My voice was low and sounded despondent, even to me. I could feel him staring at me, but I didn't dare turn my eyes to him. If I did, I had a feeling I might not be able to run when the time came. I had to remind myself that he had kidnapped me. What if the king he wanted me to heal was a terrible man? What if they planned on swooping down into my lands and killing my people? I sighed softly. The people. If I were honest with myself, I'd admit that they had never accepted my family.

"Your parents?" His voice held a note of hope. I braced myself because if I didn't, tears would fall. Shaking my head, I bit my bottom lip to keep my silence. He softly stroked my hair. And as I tried to remain quiet, I found this well inside, wanting to burst forth. Glancing over, I found his eyes full of concern. Spirits help me. He was not what I thought he'd be. Closing my eyes a moment, I tried to speak of it as if I were talking about someone else. "As you wish. My father had gone off hunting. My mother and I were high on the mountain, gathering herbs. When we came back, we discovered that his horse had thrown him and he had died. There was nothing we could do. My uncle blamed my mother. But what could she do? He was already dead. My mother…"

I took a deep, shaking breath and closed my eyes again. He pulled me to his side, and I could feel his warmth seeping into my bones. The woodsy and cinnamon scent of his body surrounded me. I was surprised that something tight in my chest—something that I had not realized had been there my whole life—suddenly uncoiled. The strength to finish my story filled me. "My mother could not bear to be alone. One day, when I went to gather plants, she took a bunch of helvan. When I got back, she was already long dead."

"How old were you?"

I let out a short, rueful laugh. "Fortunately, I was eighteen. They still tried to take the house from me even though I was of age."

He arched an eyebrow. "Did they, now?"

I smirked. "Senna is a midwife and the wife of our priest. She's been trying to get rid of my family for years. I'm sure she's very happy now."

Torric removed the meat from the fire and gave me one of the cooked hares. It was plain, but good. I'd have to take care of the cooking soon if I wanted any seasoning.

I chewed thoughtfully, watching him. If I stayed much longer, that is. "What about your parents?"

"My mother relocated to the border of your lands. It's safer there. My father died in the raid — the same raid in which our King was poisoned. We don't know how someone got close enough to poison him, he hadn't even been cut."

I paused in my meal and then turned my eyes to him. "I'm sorry."

He smiled sadly. "Thank you."

We finished our meal in companionable silence.

Afterward, I bundled up in the quilt and watched him as he put his sword to his waist. I tilted my head, curious. "Where are you going?"

He smiled. "Don't worry, lass. I'm just going to scout the area, make sure we're alone before we sleep."

Nodding, I curled up on my side and let my eyes watch the flames flicker in the night. I knew he'd keep me safe. I actually wasn't afraid of him hurting me. The question was, did I want to leave? Also, was my heart safe with him? For reasons I did not understand, I felt drawn to him, and the struggle to ignore that fact was constant.

I drifted off, only to wake some time during the night. When I sat up, I found Torric on the other side of the fire, snoring deeply. This was my chance. I didn't know where I'd go, but I had to try. The trouble was, as I looked at him, I found that I didn't want to leave his side. Something about this man was captivating, and fire flooded my heart as I gazed at him. He was powerful, and I had no doubt he would defend me, protect me. But what was I to him but a means to an end? He wanted me to heal his king. If I did that, could it end up harming my own people? As much as I felt like an outcast, as much as I questioned if they were my people, they were the only people I had ever known.

Rising quietly, I stepped lightly as I made my way out of our little campsite. If I went for the horses, I worried he'd hear me. Taking a deep breath, I glanced around. I wasn't sure where I was, but if I could get to another village, they could direct me back to Vella. Fear shook me, and I paused while shivers rolled through me. I bit my lip — now was the time to move out. Shoving my courage into my heart, I headed out down the path. It was dark, and the night enveloped me in its cool blackness as I left the flickering light of the fire. I wasn't sure where I was going, and so I stumbled as my eyes adjusted. Glancing up at the stars, I wondered how sailors read them and could tell the direction they were going. They were a mystery to me. A beautiful mystery.

The moon was high and full, which was fortunate because it helped me to see the path I was traveling. Still, the further I got from Torric, the more fear filled my heart. In the night, I could hear the sound of wolves. I silently beseeched the Spirits to keep the animals far away from me. Each noise seemed to spur on the dread that was growing in my chest.

There was a snap of twigs; I froze. My eyes darted around, but all had become quiet. Too quiet. I quelled a whimper and pressed on. If I was going to escape Torric, I could not allow terror to freeze me. This was my chance. He was asleep. On I moved, silently pushing branches out of the way. Farther and farther, I marched from the safety of Torric.

Silence filled the night. And then, there was a growl in the dark. For a moment, I stood still. And then, I was running. Behind me, I could hear a crashing through the underbrush. I didn't know what it was — but if it caught me, I knew I'd be dead.

I pushed myself to move faster, as fast as my feet could carry me. My green skirt tripped me up around my legs and so I pulled it high as I could. My heart hammered in my chest so wildly I thought that the creature giving chase could hear it. I glanced behind to see if I could catch a glimpse of it. And that was my mistake. I tripped and fell. Ankle throbbing, I rose to try to continue running. But I was too late. There, in front of me, were two large, gray wolves. Slobber dripped from their mouths in large drops as they stared at me. Behind me, I could hear the growl of another as it slowly approached, but I dared not look. I let out a wild scream and turned to the left to flee. I broke through the bushes, as branches clawed at me. Behind me, I could hear the pack giving chase. I bolted, but I knew I would not make it. Still, I shoved aside doubt and the pain in my ankle and I pressed on.

And then suddenly, I slammed into a hard chest and turned my face up to meet fierce, emerald eyes.

"Get behind me." His harshly spoken words filled me with a sense of well-being. Before I could respond, he whirled me behind him, his sword drawn as he dashed in among the wolves. Slashing and whirling, he was like a man possessed. The three wolves surrounded him and dashed at him. As his sword sliced across the muzzle of one and dug into the side of another, his other hand, armed with a hunting knife, plunged into the third. He ripped the knife out and skittered out of the jaws of the first wolf before he plunged his blade into him. It happened so fast that, for a brief moment, I couldn't comprehend it was over.

The need to heal filled my soul and a wolf whimpered. Crazed with need, I reached out to heal it when suddenly a strong arm dragged me away. I struggled against him, but he whispered softly in my ear, "No you don't. If you heal it, it will try to kill us. Come on. Let's go back."

He took my hand and started to trot back to the camp. I stumbled along, and my ankle pulsated. He turned to look at me, and my gait must have shown my weakness, for he drew me to him and whisked me up, hoisting me onto his shoulder as if I weighed nothing. On he trudged through the woods and I was lost.

Hanging there, I realized I had lost my chance to flee, and he would be much more cautious with me now. When we arrived at the camp, I expected him to dump me unceremoniously down by the fire. Instead, he gently set me onto a log and reached for my foot. He paused. "May I check your ankle?"

I blinked, surprised, and nodded mutely.

Tenderly, he lifted up my skirt high enough to get a hold of my foot. His hands carefully pressed on the bones, checking me. After a time, he looked up at me with a smile. "It isn't broken. I'll wrap it for you."

I watched him, curious. He went into one of my grandmother's boxes and pulled out some cloth bandages. Coming back to me, he wrapped my ankle with great care, and still he did not speak harshly or reprimand me in any way. When he finished, he grabbed my quilt and he wrapped me up in it. Trembling, I stared at him with wide eyes, just waiting. Finally, I couldn't take it anymore. "Aren't you going to say something?"

He took a deep breath. Watching me quietly for a moment, I fidgeted in place, feeling exposed under his gaze. Then he growled, "I'm angry, and I'm worried that if I say something, I'll scare you."

I shuddered. "I'm sorry!"

He let out a short, humorless laugh. "I'm not angry at you. I'm angry with myself. I should've known you'd try to escape. It's only natural. I should've tied you up. Or not fallen asleep. If I hadn't woken up when I did and gone after you…I almost wasn't on time!"

He stared at me, and I realized that the horror coloring his eyes was for what might have been. I whispered, "You… worried for me?"

"Yes!"

I scooted closer to him and rested my hand softly on his chest. His heart thundered under my palm, and I raised my gaze to him. He looked down at me, his eyes a war of rage, desire, and worry. "You're angry at yourself?" I asked.

He nodded, and I gently touched his cheek. He closed his eyes and nuzzled his cheek into my fingertips. A soft sigh escaped his lips. For a moment, my heart melted. If he hadn't come, I would be dead right now. I didn't think about the fact that he took me because, at that moment, it didn't matter.

And he must have seen something in my eyes, because suddenly his lips crashed down onto mine. I quivered madly as his tongue ran along the seam of my mouth, parted my lips, and slipped inside, stroking my tongue. Fire flooded my veins as I clumsily returned his kiss. There was a high-pitched noise and I realized that I was squeaking. It must have spurned him on, because I was soon on my back. His hand grasped my hip, dragging me to him as the fingers of his other hand entwined with mine and pinned me down. I whimpered and squirmed, suddenly fully aware of the hard planes of his body and the fullness of his need for me. My own core ignited in response. His kiss was hot and hungry, and even though I was not sure what I was doing, I found myself responding wildly to him.

And then, just as suddenly as it started, he was off me and backing away. I stared up at him with wide eyes. Confused, as I was left wondering if I had imagined what had happened. But I was still on my back, and his warmth was slowly leaving my body. So I knew it had been real. I sat up and stared at him.

His gruff voice tracked fire through my veins. "I shouldn't have done that. You're inexperienced, and you just tried to run from me. I came in hopes of finding a healer and bringing him or her to my king. I can't take advantage of you like that."

He strode over to the other side of the camp and sat down. I stared at him as he settled, wrapping himself in my old blanket. I felt bereft. And muddled. Why would I want him so much? Why was there still fire in my veins for him even as he sat there, staring into the dying embers of our campfire? I wanted to ask him so many things, but I didn't know where to start. So I curled in on myself and huddled under the quilt. For a while, I just watched him. After he tossed on a couple of logs, he stared into the rising flames, his brow furrowed in thought. Taking a deep breath, I turned my gaze to the flames as well.

"Sleep. I'll watch over you. I'll let nothing happen to you, Zianya. You're safe, lass. I'll protect you. Even from me." I curled up on my side. I didn't think sleep would come. But I was wrong. Eventually, the excitement of what had occurred wore off and I was exhausted. As I drifted, I swore I heard him say, "Sleep well, my Zianya."

Chapter Four

Five days. Five days passed after the kiss, and Torric still did not sit close to me. When we rode, he kept both hands on the reins and did not pull me tight to his chest. I found the whole thing confusing. A few times, I sensed he wanted to talk about it, but instead, we spoke of other things. I taught him what I knew of the plants around us; he told me about training to be a warrior. Yet, there were things he didn't tell me. He didn't tell me about the enemy they fought. He didn't tell me his place within the armies that kept this darkness at bay. And he didn't tell me more about the healers of his lands. I found myself curious. Why was he not telling me? What was going on in Kingshold?

"Will you tell me about the king?"

He was quiet for a moment and I sighed, holding onto the pommel of the saddle for balance. I began to wonder if he'd speak when he suddenly started, "The King of Glane, Donner the Just, is an honorable man. He's held together our lands for a long time, as did his father before him."

I smiled. "Do you know him?"

Again, there was a long pause before he simply said, "Yes."

"Then let me ask you again. What is the King of Glane like?"

"Donner has a mischievous sense of humor that he rarely shows. He's very affectionate with his wife and cares greatly for his children. His greatest hope is to end this war so that our land can heal. He's the only healer left in Glane, and it kills him that he can't go out there and tend to his warriors. Not to mention, because he can't heal himself, right now he's under great pressure."

I paused for a moment, letting his words sink in. Then I asked, "How is it you know him so well?"

"My only sister is his wife."

My eyes grew wide. "Really?"

"Really."

My eyes drifted along the trail ahead of us. Large trees lined the path, and the rich green of the forest surrounded us. The air was unseasonably cool and felt as if soon it would be fall. I'd miss not seeing the colors as they changed. I greatly doubted I would be able to leave once I healed the king, no matter how honorable he was. But more importantly, how was it that the king's brother-in-law was here in this land? I also wondered why, even though he knew some things, he didn't know more about the needs of healers.

"How come you didn't know about the dietary requirements of a healer?"

I could hear the smile in his voice. "I was a child when my grandmother died. Also, do you think my king would allow people to know such a weakness? Besides, he hasn't healed anyone as far as I know. He can't, he once told me. Now I know why. He probably is afraid to be out cold when our people need him most."

Tilting my head, I glanced up at him. "Do you have any more siblings?"

"No."

I laughed lightly at the short answer and pressed on. "Well, what is your sister's name?"

"Sarine. She's sweet, with hair as black as mine and the same green eyes. She's currently carrying their third child. When we were little, she was always reading books and dreaming of adventures."

"That sounds like me," I said softly before I let my eyes roam to the mountains ahead of us. I knew we were heading toward the Pass of Winds. What I wondered was how he intended to get past the guards with me. From what I knew of the Pass, there was a contingent of guards protecting us from the barbarians of the West. But I also knew at least one warrior of Glane had made it all the way to Vella. The proof was sitting behind me. I let out a long, slow breath.

"What are you thinking of, lass?"

"Too many things."

He chuckled. As a responding smile took me, I realized I loved how easy it was for him to do so.

Curiosity colored his voice as he said, "Well, pick one and we'll start with that."

My lips twisted as I drew forth my courage and whispered, "Since you kissed me, you've barely touched me. Why is that?"

I surprised myself at my own directness. It wasn't like me at all, but it had been my obsession these last five days. He froze and remained quiet for a long time. After a while, I didn't think he'd speak of it. But I was wrong. "I kidnapped you, took you from your home. I shouldn't be taking advantage of you. That's what I did."

I tilted my head to look up at him again. "So you are a man of honor."

He grinned down at me. "I am. Or at least, I'd like to think so."

"Will I ever see home again?"

For a moment, his hand left the reins and I thought he'd embrace me. Instead, he returned his hand to the leather length and clutched it. Gently, he said, "Do you really wish to go back to people who treat you as if you were a witch? My people," —he shook his head—"our people, Zianya, will treat you kindly. If you help our king, you'll have a place of honor amongst our people."

I leaned back into his warmth and sighed, "*Our* people?"

"You know as well as I that your great-grandmother must have come from Glane."

The surety of his words rang true, but still, I resisted the idea. "I don't know that."

Finally, he wrapped his arm around me and hugged me to his chest. I felt cozy and secure. A breath I hadn't realized I was holding let loose, and I relaxed into him. His arm tightened around me. For a long while, we rode like that. I hadn't understood how much I had missed his holding me until that moment.

Gently, he whispered in my ear, "You do know that."

He went to remove his arm, but I clung to it and held it to me. "I like it there. I feel…safer."

His rich, warm laugh filled my senses. "As you wish, lass."

For a time, we rode on in silence. The heat of his chest seeped into my back and filled me with a sense of contentment. My mind rolled over that kiss—and the intense fire that had filled me—again. Would it be wrong to fall for the man who'd kidnapped me? He wasn't like a normal kidnapper. I smiled. Not that I knew what one was like.

"Why do you smile?"

A deep flush filled my cheeks. "Never mind. How long will it take us to get to Kingshold?"

"If we only stop to rest, about six more weeks, so long as we don't run into trouble. But if the wolves are any indication, you may be the type to attract trouble." His voice teasingly caressed my ear.

I giggled in his arms and he squeezed me to him. Once again, we rode like that. It was easy to fall into a relaxed rhythm with him. I didn't understand what I was feeling. Back home, I had spent as little time as I could with the men of my village. It was hard to have any sort of emotions for men who called you a demon spawn when they thought you weren't listening. Even as a child, I'd avoided others. Yet, here I was in this stranger's arms, feeling more at home than I ever had in my twenty-two years.

"You should let me season our meat before you cook it. If you packed my jars, I'm sure I've got some stuff for seasoning."

I could hear the grin in his voice. "Disliking my food already?"

"No." I did not want to mention that sometimes it was badly cooked. "Well. It is a bit plain. Yet, I'm sure that's only because you don't have anything for seasoning."

He snickered in my ear. "Even if I had some, I wouldn't know what to do. You can season the food, and I'll cook it."

"May I ask why you won't just have me cook?"

"If you burn yourself, you can't heal yourself. If I burn myself, you can heal me."

Satisfaction filled me and an easy smile took my lips. There it was again—a feeling as if I should be with him. It was hard to explain it. I wasn't sure I'd ever understand it. Yet, something in the back of my mind had made me feel that I belonged with him ever since I first felt his lips on mine. I couldn't comprehend it. And if I was being honest, if he pressed me, I might have been too afraid to notice it. But right then, in his arms, it just felt…right.

It had been a little over a week and a half since my kidnapping when I asked, "Should we stop at a village to get more bread and cheese? Maybe some other staples? We're out."

He was quiet for a long while.

So finally, I pressed. "Well?"

"Lass, Vella is unusual in that they didn't kill your great-grandmother."

I blinked as I let those softly spoken words hover between us. And then reality sank in. Gasping, I could feel sorrow pierce my soul. My heart suddenly fluttered in pain, but still, I pressed on because I had to be certain. "How do you know this?"

His arm tightened around me. He was quiet as his horse picked its way along the path. It was barely a path and I wondered how often it saw use.

My eyes roamed the area and then I turned to him. "How?" The pain in his eyes as he looked down at me filled me with a sense of dread. He knew something, and it had to be terrible. I slipped my hand over his and squeezed softly. I said one soft word: "Please."

He turned his eyes away and spoke gently. "I questioned a few villagers along the way. It wasn't easy — if they looked too closely at my eyes, they'd run from me. But when I got someone to speak, it was always the same thing: they'd burned the witches as they came over the border ninety years ago. The only reason I kept going was a rumor that Vella kept a witch as a slave. My intention was to rescue you. I thought you'd be grateful. I didn't expect you to have your own home when I found you. I was thankful that you seemed to be free and well, even if I regretted that I had to kidnap you."

I took in a shaky breath and felt pressure behind my eyes. Tears were close and I fought them. But how could I not cry for all those men and women who had died simply because they were like me? I clung to his arm and then quaked when I started to sob violently. All that wasted life. That could have been my great-grandmother.

If Senna had had her way, that could have been me.

Hot lips brushed my ear as he whispered, "Hush now, lass. This is why I didn't want to tell you."

"It's just so wrong!" I wailed. "The healers of Glane escaped only to be slaughtered by my people. How can you not want to take revenge?"

His body stiffened against my back and it took him a moment before his breathing calmed enough to speak. "Trust me, lass, there's a part of me that does. But my first mission is to bring you home. King Donner needs you. And after all this time, whom would it help? I'd be murdering innocent people."

For a stretch, we continued to ride in silence, tears dripping down my cheeks. Yet, soon, it was getting to be late afternoon, and Torric found us a place to camp for the night. As he went hunting for something to eat, I searched through my boxes until I found some seasoning. If we had a pot, I could have made us a stew. That would at least be something different. Although properly cooked some days, most days it was badly cooked meat over an open fire, and that was starting to get to me. There had to be something we could do.

When Torric returned, I rubbed the seasoning into the wild game hen he had caught. He watched me with a soft gaze, and I tried to avoid the worry I saw in his eyes. It seemed that he no longer feared me running after my near-wolf attack. Truth was, that I was not interested in trying to run from him again. It may have been because there was something unspoken between us since that day, and now there was this yearning in my blood that I didn't understand.

My face finally dry from all the tears, he smiled at me and I could feel my cheeks brighten into a deep red.

"You look rather fetching when you blush," he said.

I laughed. "Hush!"

His grin broadened. "I'm only admitting a truth, lass."

A nervous giggle slipped from me, and I turned my gaze out into the woods. As I did, I thought about how we were now living on whatever he could hunt. Trouble was, I needed more food than normal people did. A few leftover bits of meat weren't going to sustain me if this went on. If we could get flour, oil, and a few other staples, I could last. Glancing over at him, I wondered if he could trust me enough to do this. "We're going to need more food."

He eyed me quietly. Finally, he said, "Lass, I don't know what you want me to do."

"Let's go fairly close to a village. I'll stay out of it, hidden in the forest. You could trade a few of my herbs, or sell some of my creams or something. If you could get flour, oil, some other basics, and a pot and pan, we could eat better."

"Lass, I can hunt enough food for us."

I sighed. "I won't run, if that's your worry."

His deep voice tore from him. "You think that's what I fear? What I fear, Zianya, is one of those villagers getting their hands on you. Do you know what they'll do to you?"

"I'll stay hidden, I promise. The trouble is that I can't be missing a meal. If I truly have to heal you at some point, I'll need a lot of food. If you can get the right supplies, we don't have to rely solely on your hunting skills."

Thoughtful eyes stared at me. I could see him debating it in his eyes. If he had taken me after my market day, I would have had a fully stocked kitchen for him to raid. But when he took me, all I had was four loaves of seed bread, butter, and a cheese wheel.

Finally, he nodded. "All right. Tomorrow, I'll bring us closer to a village. You'll stay hidden deep in the woods. Don't come out. I'll go in and out as quickly as I can."

I smiled at him. "I'll make a list of things we need and how much to sell each item we're going to barter. I'll also write down what they're used for."

He frowned. "There's a trouble with that, lass."

"What's that?"

"As strange as it may seem, while our spoken tongue is the same, our written language is completely different."

I blinked in surprise. "What?"

He nodded, and I sighed as I remembered my great-grandmother had bought those books to learn the *written* language of Renth. There was too much to tell him, I had to write it down. I wondered if he could write it down but as I looked through my belongings, I realized we had no writing supplies. What could we do?

I looked at him. There was one thing, but he wasn't going to like it. "Then I need to go."

"No!" His eyes flashed and the emerald color churned with his unspoken thoughts.

"Listen. You brought my shawl. I'll braid my hair so that it isn't in my face, and then I'll drape the shawl over my head and hide my hair. My eyebrows are fairly dark, so no one should notice."

"And our eyes?"

"Well, if we both put in a drop of aliin in each eye, our eyes will sting, but they'll also take on a muddy color."

He frowned at me. "That can't be good for our eyes."

I sighed. "Technically, it isn't. But once we leave the village, I'll heal your eyes."

"And your eyes? I love your pretty shade of jade."

"I...I don't know. They'll take back their color, though."

"But?"

"But...it might damage my eyesight."

"Permanently?"

Softly, I replied, "I don't know. If it damages my eyesight, then the only thing that can repair it is another healer. And since your king won't heal...I don't know what to say."

His jaw tightened. "We'll figure something else out."

I shook my head. "There's nothing to figure out. This is what we'll do. It won't blind me completely; I'll still be able to function. The chances of it happening are very slim," I lied with a skill that amazed me. "Most likely, it won't happen. We have to do this. I need the extra food."

I carefully left out the fact that if it did damage me, I'd be in pain for a long time. Instinctively, I knew that he'd never let me do this if he had that knowledge. He thought about it for a while, but finally, he relented. I could see it in his eyes before he even spoke.

"Fine. But only because you really need the food."

The next day, we veered from our usual course and headed toward the nearest village. Torric was nervous—I could feel it in the tension in his arm around my waist and in the pounding of his heart against my back. I didn't expect him to be nervous. He had taken all those wolves on with no fear. Then it struck me—he was afraid for me. I stroked his arm. "I'll be safe. I'll be with you."

He clutched me to his chest. A few hours away from the village, we dropped in the aliin. It stung, and I let out a little whimper once it was over. Torric swore. Biting my bottom lip, I braced myself so that I wouldn't make another sound. After that, I wrapped my shawl around me, making sure my tightly braided red hair was covered.

When we got to the village, it was much like Vella, with the red walls, gates, and roofs. Toward the center, I could even see a temple rising above the others. I smiled because it had a familiar feeling. But the smile soon left my face as I realized that these people would probably burn me.

When we got to the gate, I let Torric do the talking as he explained we were trading for supplies. The guards at the gate allowed us entry, and we followed the constable's directions to the market. When we arrived, I let my eyes roam over the area. Vendors bartered with various customers, some calling out their wares, causing a cacophony of noise. I smiled brightly at Torric as he got me off the horse. Grabbing onto the reins of the packhorse, I made my way to the official apothecary. Vella used to have an apothecary until my grandmother put him out of business. Selling my wares to a reseller meant that I wouldn't be able to get full price, but once the apothecary saw the quality of my goods, I'd still be able to get a decent one.

Delight and surprised filled me when I realized the apothecary was a woman. From her eyes, I could tell Torric enchanted her, so I introduced him as my brother.

With a relaxed smile, the woman with graying brown hair asked, "So, Torric, have you a wife at home?"

My eyes darted to him. He hadn't mentioned one to me before, but I was curious nonetheless. His now muddy colored eyes darted to me before he smiled at the apothecary and said, "No, I've not settled yet."

Her eyes lit up. "You must come to my home after the market. My daughter, Lyla, is lovely and sweet."

"We'd loved to," I chimed in. I could feel Torric's eyes on me and I suppressed the need to grin as we chatted with her for a time, and I was happy that Torric played along. Finally, we got down to business, and I was grateful because my eyes were aching by the time the money we needed was in my hand. The pain shooting through my head seemed intent on bursting forth. It took everything for me to feign wellness.

As we walked away, Torric said, "Brother?"

"It softened her up," I replied softly.

"Yes," he said, his voice tinged with surliness, "but now she wants us to stop by her home after the market so I can meet her daughter."

I laughed under my breath, which was a mistake as fresh spikes of pain shot through me. Suppressing a groan, I said, "Don't worry. We're going to get what we need and get out of here. How are your eyes?"

"Burning."

Worry stained his gaze as he assessed me, and I smiled, trying to convince him that I was well. Keeping my voice light, I said, "As soon as we exit the village, I'll fix them for you."

After that, we moved among the stalls and bought what we needed. I let Torric do most of the haggling and he was surprisingly good at it. While he did that, the throbbing in my head only increased. I had a feeling it had to do with the aliin. I silently implored whatever Spirit was listening that to make the pain wear off. But as we made our way among the stalls, it only worsened.

When we got to the end of the vendors, I assumed he was going to put me on the horse, but then he stopped. I looked up at him, confused. For a long moment, he stared at me with a contemplative gaze, and then he smiled at me. "Wait here. I forgot something."

"What did you . . ."

Too late. He was gone.

As I waited, a couple of young men came over to me. I tried to ignore them, but they stopped and grinned down at me. I shifted nervously and then jumped when one said softly in my ear, "You're a pretty little thing. Why are you all covered up?"

My head ringing, I attempted strength as I said, "My husband prefers me that way. He doesn't like people looking at what's his."

The taller of the two leered at me. "If you were my woman, I'd show you everywhere."

"Well, as I said — I'm married."

The shorter man leaned close again and whispered greedily, "That's never stopped me before."

I stiffened and felt his hand tightly clench my upper arm. Wiggling, I tried to pull out of his grasp, but he laughed as he dragged me close to his body. Fear turned my veins to ice, and the pounding in my head increased. I braced myself and turned to him. "My husband will be here soon."

The two of them laughed. "We'd better hurry then."

He tugged on me to haul me away, and I gripped the reins of the horses tighter as I cried out, "Let me go!"

"What are you doing with my woman?"

The harsh roar of Torric's voice filled me with ease. I fixed my eyes on him and smiled at the intensity of his gaze. His hand rested lightly on his sword as he glared at the two men.

Suddenly, my arm was free.

"Sorry. We didn't know she was with you."

Once they were out of sight, I looked up to find Torric giving me a wry grin. I tilted my head and opened my mouth to ask what he was staring at when he said, "As I said, trouble is attracted to you."

I blushed and he lifted me into the saddle. Swinging up behind me, he hauled me close and then we quickly made our way out of the village. The moment it was out of sight, I grasped his hand to heal him. My head pounded from my stinging eyes, but I was determined he'd have a clear head. I could tell he was about to speak to stop me, but I pressed forward, letting the healing flow from me. Once his eyes were fine, the sweet oblivion of sleep reached for me and I gratefully let it take me.

Chapter Five

The first thing I noticed was the throbbing in my head. My eyes felt like grains of sand were coating them. I let out a moan and when I did, a soft hand stroked my cheek. My grimy eyes opened, and I found Torric looking down at me with worry. I tried to smile and sit up.

He pushed me back down gently. "How do you feel?"

"Like someone clubbed me over the head. I'm hungry, and I could use some tayden tea for my headache. Maybe a wet cloth for my eyes?"

He leaned close to me and stared into my eyes. He frowned. "Your eyes are jade again, but they're bloodshot. I'll get you a cloth and then I'll get some food for you."

"We bought some bread and cheese, too, so could you get me that to nibble on while you get the meat going?"

He laughed softly. "You do know I got us some eggs and bacon. I'm going to make you that this morning."

I stretched with a long yawn. Flinching, I realized that was a mistake. Still, I said softly, "Sounds good." Drawing air into my lungs, I forced myself to stand and I made my way towards the wooden boxes while Torric searched the sack of hay that contained our eggs.

"Hey, sit back down. I'll get what you need."

A twist of a smile flickered at my lips despite the pain. "Do you know what tayden tea looks like?"

He frowned. "No."

"Exactly."

Crouching down, I opened one of the boxes and rummaged through it until I found the tea. I placed a small amount into a little mesh satchel and tied it up. I was glad to find my eyesight was unaffected, even if my encrusted eyes were scratchy and my head pounded like a horse was galloping on it. I grabbed a tin cup and put the satchel into it. Sitting back down, I smiled gratefully up at Torric as he poured some hot water into the cup from our newly acquired kettle, and gave me a wet cloth. I put it on my eyes and then closed them, hoping to ease some of the pain while waiting for the tea to steep.

Soon the smell of bacon and eggs filled the air, and the promise of cold bread and cheese no longer seemed appealing. After a few moments, I gently rubbed my eyes with the wet cloth and then I started to sip the tea. I knew it wouldn't bring immediate relief, but I also knew it would help me soon enough.

"How does that taste?"

I smiled up at him. "Bitter."

He handed me a tin plate with surprisingly perfectly cooked scrambled eggs and bacon on it. He even had toasted some bread in the pan. Studying him, I was glad to see the emerald in his eyes had returned. Although, concern filled them and that reddened my cheeks. Instead, I focused on what was in front of me and took a bite of eggs. I let out a satisfied moan. "The tea is bitter, as it should be. The eggs, on the other hand, are divine."

He sat next to me and dug into his own food. As I ate and drank the tea, the headache lessened but did not go. It was right behind my eyes. I had one of those rare moments where I wished I could heal myself. I needed it. My eyes traveled to Torric of their own accord and then I tore them away. I didn't know how long this dull ache would last. I just hoped it cleared up soon.

After we ate, he gathered everything and went to the river to wash it. I burrowed into my grandmother's quilt and sipped some more tea. I had a feeling the dull ache behind my eyes would last a few more days at least. When he returned, he broke camp, and then gently lifted me onto the horse before swinging up behind me as usual. I leaned back into him and closed my eyes.

"Why don't you try to sleep?" he asked.

So over the course of the next few days, I slept more than I ever had in my life. I could tell Torric was worried, and so I spent part of each day reassuring him I'd be fine after some rest. When I was awake, we'd talk about the little things: I preferred cats, and he liked dogs. When I told him my favorite color was blue, he told me his favorite was jade-green. That had set my cheeks on fire. They were silly things, but I felt closer to him as we continued on our journey.

On the fourth day, I felt better. It had now been sixteen days since I left my home. I smiled. More like taken. Trouble kicked around in my heart as I realized that his kidnapping didn't bother me anymore. I simply wasn't sure what type of person that made me. But there were things that I understood. Torric was a powerful man who had possibly killed before, but he was gentle with me. He didn't look upon me as some evil to tolerate. Then there was the other thing — he still hadn't kissed me again. It took me a while, but I had come to the realization that he was trying to show me respect by not doing it again. I found myself studying his lips a great deal until I realized I was craving his kiss. I had no idea how to get him to do it again. My lack of experience made me shy.

So instead of asking him to kiss me, I leaned back into his arms to absorb the heat of his chest on my back. I held my hand over his on my waist, and I wondered what my new home would be like. Sometimes, my heart would flutter unhappily at the idea that once we were there — after I'd healed his king — I would never see him again. Whatever it was building between us eluded me. Oddly enough, a part of me hoped that whatever it was would grow and last. And that part of me desperately wished that hope wasn't misplaced.

As we were riding, with me resting in his warm embrace, his hard body suddenly stiffened. I glanced up at him. A deep frown took his face, and his emerald eyes darted around the forest that surrounded us. I turned my own eyes toward it and glanced around. I couldn't see anything, but the forest did seem unusually quiet. For a time, we rode on and nothing happened. After a bit, he brought the horses up to a canter and we moved quickly. As darkness fell, we continued our ride when normally we'd camp. When my stomach growled, he gave a little laugh and then pulled some bread and cheese out of the saddlebag and handed it to me. I glanced up at him. "Aren't you going to eat?"

"When we stop for the night."

I chewed on some seed bread and sighed softly. "Are we going to stop for the night? You seem…I don't know. Something's wrong."

Leaning down, he kissed my brow and said, "Not to worry, lass. I'll protect you."

I thrilled at the brief contact. He smiled down at me. It was obvious that he was trying to comfort me. Make me feel safe. And as I thought about that, I started to get nervous. I gazed down the moonlit path. Quickly, I finished my food, but it sat heavily in my stomach.

At some point, I must have drifted off because I woke to him lifting me off the saddle. He held me close in his arms and I stared up at him. My eyes drifted to his full lips for a long moment before I stared up into his eyes with a deep sense of yearning. He swore softly as he gently set me down. "If you keep looking at me like that, lass, I'll not be able to hold back from kissing you."

"What if I don't want you to hold—"

Capturing my lips in a rush, he drowned out my words. Heat and a deep need tracked through my veins until they ignited my core as he slowly and thoroughly kissed me. I didn't know how much time had passed, but I shivered as he clutched me tightly to him. I was hesitant at first, but then I pressed my lips to his, shyly letting my tongue tease his mouth. His mouth opened and his tongue met mine hungrily. A soft sound escaped my throat as his hand slid down to my backside and grasped my bottom, drawing me closer to the hard length of his body. Then he slowly, languidly, gave me soft kiss after soft kiss. When it was over, my eyes opened to find him smiling down at me. My cheeks flushed and I turned away shyly. One of his hands softly took my face and angled it back toward him. Huskily, he said, "Never turn from me, Zianya. You've no reason to feel shy with me."

"It's just…I've never kissed anyone before you."

He smiled and kissed my brow. "Oh, I know that. I told you the first time I kissed you I knew you were inexperienced."

I let out a huff, and my cheeks must have turned an even darker shade of red because he laughed. "Your lack of experience with men is something I like about you, lass. Trust me when I say many men enjoy being the first with a woman. Knowing they're the first to touch her, claim her. No need to be embarrassed. But it's something to remind me that I need to take things slowly with you. I don't want to overwhelm you, and I don't want you to feel like you have no choice but to be with me."

It was my turn to laugh before surprising myself by boldly saying, "That isn't it. I don't understand what it is, but I feel like being with you, in your arms, is where I was meant to be."

He stroked my hair back. "I understand what you mean. Come on. Let's get the camp together for the night. I want to be out of here before dawn."

I studied him for a long moment. Then I asked, "What are you worried about?"

"Don't worry. I won't let anything happen to you."

I sighed. "Torric, you're worried. You may not let anything happen to me, but I worry about something happening to you."

The tenderness of his smile had my toes tingling. It was more than just a desire to kiss him—I felt warm and safe in his arms. I adored listening to his laugh, and the idea of parting from him wounded my heart. I didn't think I was in love with him, but I suspected that I might have been falling for him. "Don't worry, Zianya. I'll keep myself safe, too. After all, you need me to protect you. I don't want to leave you alone."

An emotion I didn't quite recognize filled my heart, and I moved on to get dinner going while he went to get water from the nearby river. I hoped that the rest of our journey would keep us near it. As I seasoned the food, I poured my heart into singing an old tune that my grandmother used to sing to me when I was young about a warrior and his young bride and his promise to return to her. I was so into the song that I didn't even sense Torric when he arrived with the water.

He startled me when he said, "How do you know that song?"

I glanced back at him and then returned to finish off cutting the wild chicken he'd killed earlier into chunks before I answered, "My grandmother used to sing it to me. Why?"

"That song comes from Glane. My mother used to sing it all the time."

I took the pot of water from him and smiled. "Just more evidence that my healer great-grandmother came from there. I'm pretty sure my grandmother learned it from her."

After he finished off the cooking, we ate sitting very close to one another. I could feel his warmth all down my right side where our bodies touched. However, he didn't kiss me again. I suspected he didn't want to spook me. What he didn't realize was that his earlier kiss had only made me long for more.

When we finished, he took everything to wash by the river. I pulled out my grandmother's quilt—which was looking a little worse for wear—and wrapped myself up in it.

When he came back, I shyly lifted one side of the quilt in invitation. His eyes filled with surprise...and then, hot desire. He walked up to me and stared down into my eyes for a long moment before he gently guided my hand to wrap back around myself. Sitting next to me outside of the blanket, he slipped an arm around me and held me close. "Go to sleep. I'll keep watch."

"Aren't you going to sleep?"

"Not this night. It's going to get cold. I'm not going to put more wood on the fire. So stay close."

Burrowing into his side, I rested my head on his shoulder. His lips brushed my brow, and I sighed in contentment. I slipped one hand free of the quilt and softly laid it against his chest, over his heart. He shuddered once, his heart thundered, and he drew me tighter to him. Softly, he started singing to me the same tune. The words were the same, but this included a final verse about the warrior being lost without his True Mate and how he was not whole until he returned to her. I felt my whole body melt into his side, and I knew that wherever he was, I was safe.

"Zianya," a husky voice whispered in my ear. I opened my eyes and it was dark. The fire was nothing but dim coals. If it wasn't for the moon, I would not have been able to see at all. I turned my gaze up to find Torric looking out into the night, his face hard. Something was definitely wrong. "Lass, when I tell you, I want you to run."

I whispered back, "I'll not leave you."

Crouching next to me, he said, "Lass, I can defend you better if you go hide. Here, take this."

He pressed a sheathed blade into my hand. I stared at him, fear prickling my insides. I had never used a dagger before. "What do you expect me to do with this?"

"Hopefully nothing. It'll make me feel better if you have it."

Clutching it to my chest, a tremble shuddered through me. Tears filled my eyes as I rose. He was gathering his weapons, and I leaned down and softly kissed his brow. Glancing up at me, he nodded and indicated which way to go with his eyes. I smiled down at him, my heart full. "Come back to me, my warrior."

With that, I fled. Running wildly into the woods, I begged the Spirits to protect me from whoever it was out there. Darkness enveloped me. I went to ground and turned to watch the camp. In the dim moonlight, Torric was standing with his sword at the ready. My heart fluttered furiously within my chest until I thought it would fly from me.

As I watched, I saw three men walk in to the camp. Two were tall with dark hair, one was shorter with blond hair.

"What do you want?" Torric asked, almost sounding bored.

The shorter man's voice was gruff and made me shiver as anxiousness coldly settled in my heart. "Where's the little witch in need of a burning you were riding with?"

"We parted ways. What do you want?" Torric responded, his voice steady, giving away nothing.

The blond man grinned. "Whatever you might have."

It happened so fast, I nearly missed it. Torric struck hard and fast, and then one of the two dark-haired men was down, blood soaking his chest before he fell. The other two sprang to attack, but there was an obvious difference in their skill. I didn't know much about fighting, but I could see Torric's intense training as he moved like a viper, dodging and parrying. They danced as my warrior deflected the blades of the two bandits. Suddenly, another bandit came into view. He was sneaking up behind, and I sensed he was going to attack Torric without warning.

Through the forest I crept while keeping my eye on the attacker. Torric slashed, rotated, sidestepped, and suddenly stabbed one of the men. He went down, and Torric focused on the last dark-haired man.

When I got to a certain point, I dashed out of the woods. The man sneaking up on Torric started to turn, but I jumped onto his back and plunged my blade through to his chest. Hot, wet blood covered my hand as the man went down. At the same time, I heard another thud. But it was like a dream, and I was transfixed. The need to heal rushed over me in a wave, taking all desire but one from me. The man looked up at me with wide blue eyes full of fear. Fear of death, fear of me. I took a deep breath and reached out. Before I knew it, a large arm hauled me away. "Don't. Look away, lass."

Mesmerized, my breath came in quick gasps. I stretched and strained as Torric dragged me into his warm chest. He let out a frustrated exhale and jerked me closer. Suddenly, I heard the sickening sound of metal pressing into flesh. The need to heal left me, turning around, I found Torric staring at me. He didn't look happy.

"What do you think you were doing? You could've been hurt or killed!" His voice was gruff, angry—but fear did not touch me. I knew that this was because he was worried about me.

I wasn't about to cower to this, however. Meeting his eyes I said, "I saw him sneaking up on you. I wasn't about to stand by and let him kill you!"

Gritting his teeth, his voice was still harsh from the battle as he said, "I knew he was there, he wasn't close enough to bother me.

"How was I to know that? You sent me out to run and hide. You wanted me to abandon you to an unknown fate, and I couldn't do that!" Tears filled my eyes and his gaze softened. He released his sword and softly stroked my cheek. Tenderly, gently, he kissed me, and I melted into him. Warmth and safety filled my soul, and I pressed closer to him. Too quickly, his lips left mine, leaving me feeling bereft. He smiled before telling me to pack up because we needed to get out of there.

After I quickly went to clean my hands of the blood, I gathered our things. He dragged the bodies deeper into the brush. Once the boxes were full, he set about getting them onto the packhorse. Then he lifted me up onto our horse and we set out. As we rode, the realization that I had helped take a life filled me. Silent tears sprung forth and rolled down my cheeks as shame tore at my heart like the dagger I had used. Torric held me close, and I nuzzled my head back into him until I could cry no more and fell asleep in his arms.

Chapter Six

I woke to the sound of my stomach growling, and a rich, honeyed laugh brought flames to my cheeks. My eyes darted around; I found the day was bright, and we were on the main road, such as it was.

I could almost hear the grin in Torric's voice. "Not much farther and we'll stop to eat. But I want to keep going after. If those bandits had friends, I want to put as much distance as I can between us and them."

With a nod of my head, I turned to watch the passing landscape. Over the clip-clop of the horses' hooves, I could hear the gentle gurgling of the river to our right. There were flowers lining the left side of the trail, and I had the urge to gather and dry them for tea. The air was not overly hot, but clear. The wind gently cooled my skin, which was good, because heat from Torric's tightly wrapped arm sunk into me.

Leaning against his chest, I slipped my arms around the one he had around my waist, and I clung to it. He started singing in my ear, and I felt a deep sense of peace fill me. In the past, what people had believed about me had never stopped me from standing up for myself when it was necessary. However, I had to admit that all of my life, I had been secretly nervous around people. I didn't want to see the looks they gave me or hear them call me a witch when my back was turned. So I had tried to hide from my feelings, ignoring any hurt. Until this moment, I had fought to keep myself from realizing how unhappy I was back in Vella. Perhaps Vella was not my home. Perhaps it was just where I grew up.

Eventually, we found a spot. While Torric unburdened the horses, he said we weren't going to set up a proper campsite. He did, however, get a fire going, and I got ready to help cook. Now that we had proper supplies, he wasn't as worried I'd burn myself and was willing to let me help a bit more, which was nice. I figured he didn't want to go hunting for us, so I made oatmeal from the small sack of oats we had. There were dried meats that we could eat later on the road if we got hungry again.

After we ate quietly, I quickly cleaned up the utensils and myself by the brook as he put the fire out. While I was waiting beside the horse, he came over to me and smiled. There was a strange gleam in his eyes, and I wondered what he was up to.

Softly, I asked, "Aren't you going to lift me up?" He grinned down at me before he held up a burgundy velvet satchel to me. I took it gently from him and raised my eyes. "What's this?"

His eyes danced in excitement. "I bought it for you in the village. But then you were feeling terrible for a few days and I didn't get around to it. Open it."

My heart quickened as I opened the satchel. Reaching in, I pulled out a length of leather cord with a large pendant of deep blue stone lovingly carved into a hawk in midflight. It was beautiful, each feather carefully detailed. Tears sprang to my eyes. He drew me close and held me tightly to him as I burrowed into his chest and smiled.

"It isn't much. When we get to Glane, I'll be able to get you something proper."

"*Proper*?" Confused, I leaned back and looked up into his eyes. He fell silent as he examined me, a little expectant. When I stared up at him, still confused, I could see him make a decision before he then whispered, "Let me put that on you."

My cheeks went red as I let him drape the necklace around my throat. I'd never received a gift from a man before, and I felt a thrilling shiver through my heart. Turning to him, I got up onto my toes and kissed his lips once, softly. "Thank you."

His eyes locked onto mine and he hauled me to him. Pressing his tender lips to mine, he drew me into a passionate embrace. I breathed him in and felt as if I were suddenly whole. Clinging to him, I trembled as he clutched my hips and yanked me closer. I melted into him, dizzy with desire. Then he drew away, our breaths coming in quick, heated gasps as he stared down at me. "I need to be careful with you."

I laughed. "What if I don't want you to be careful with me?"

He growled and I felt my eyes go wide as he roughly whispered, "Be careful what you say to me, little healer."

With that, he positioned me in the saddle and swung up behind me. I sunk back into his warmth as we rode on. Drawing the pendant up to examine, my breath hitched just a bit. The artisanship was beautiful. I doubted Torric knew that a blue hawk was a protection charm, but it made me happy nonetheless.

The next few days were all roughly the same. For the most part, we rode with only short breaks for the horses and me. Torric was on constant guard, so we didn't speak as much as usual. I was beginning to worry when, one day, he abruptly decided that we could camp the whole night. I stretched out as he unburdened the horses. "I think I'm going to go down to the river and bathe before we get our meal going."

He froze and his eyes turned to me. I blushed under the fiery gaze and turned away before saying, "Don't look at me like that."

His lips twisted into a frown before he said, "I don't want you going down there by yourself."

I laughed. "I'm not going to take a full bath with you watching me!"

He grinned. "Now that would be a lovely sight, lass."

"There's no one around. I'll be fine. Please?"

The grin left his face and for a long moment, Torric stared at me. Then he nodded. "Half an hour. If you're not back by then, I'm coming for you."

I felt my face light up. Dashing to him, I hugged him tightly. "Thank you! Don't worry, I'll be quick."

Going to the boxes, I dug out the lavender soap, thankful he'd grabbed it with my other jars. There was a spring in my step as I made my way to the river. As I came upon the river's bank, I noticed an inlet where the water had pooled. Deciding that was the best place for a bath, I strolled over. Before I stripped, I looked around to make sure I was alone. This would be the first real bath I'd had in a while. Prior to this, all I had been able to do was quickly clean up each day.

The water was cold but refreshing, and once I was in, I dove under and scrubbed my hair roughly. Honestly, I wondered why Torric was still flirting with me with my hair this gross. I rose from the water and sighed. Making my way to the bank, I grabbed the soap and proceeded to wash. The rich and sweet scent of lavender filled my senses and calmed my soul. Once I was clean, I soaked in the cold water. But it was too cold to stay long, and I feared Torric's arrival.

Getting out, I dried off with a sheet Torric had used to protect my jars, which I figured I would dry by the fire. After dressing, I carefully braided my hair. It was peaceful, calm, and I reveled in these quiet moments. At the sound of twigs snapping, I rose and turned with a smile. "I thought I had a little more time. I'm sorry."

Out of the woods strode two men. Fear shot through my heart like an arrow as I stared at them. One was rather short and wide, his gray hair thinning. The other man was what I would have once considered tall until I'd met Torric. He was strong, capable, with dark brown hair and brilliant blue eyes. The eyes of both sent a shiver straight to my bones.

"Um, hello. I'm Zianya."

The older man growled. "Yer a witch."

My heart fluttered wildly. "No! No, I'm not a witch, I'm a healer."

On silent steps, the younger man was next to me, and he whispered, "A witch."

Then darkness took me an instant later.

My head throbbed. I could hear scuffling near me. My mind flashed through the events that occurred before I blacked out. There had been two men. Both of who had called me a witch. I held my body very still and quiet, but my heart kicked up a rapid beat.

"I jus' want ta 'ave a li'l fun. I don' understand why yer arguin', Kree." The voice sounded young, like the last voice I heard before I'd blacked out.

"She's a witch, boy. Ya know what happens ta men that bed witches?"

There was a huff of annoyance. "No, what?"

"Their parts rot off." There was another annoyed huff of breath. "And soon after, they die a slow, miserable death."

"Well, she said she's a healer. A sexy little healer. Maybe she's that healer ya hear about from Vella."

The older man barked out a gruff laugh. "Don' be fooled. She'd say anythin' ta trick us. The moment we take our eyes off 'er, she'd've cursed us. 'Sides, what'd that healer from Vella be doin' here?"

In that moment, I was glad that they didn't realize the healer of Vella was missing. I had a feeling that if they knew that, the younger man would have raped me. Probably the older man, too. The trouble was, that only took the imminent threat of violation away. That didn't mean there was no danger. It just wasn't immediate.

"I don' know. Guess yer right. She's a witch. So what are we goin' ta do?"

I quivered, and they paused. Kree said, "She's awake. Ya may as well sit up and open yer eyes, witch."

Letting out the breath I'd been holding, I did just that. Glancing around, I saw the two of them glowering at me. Kree, the older man, regarded me with a little fear and a lot of hatred. The younger still had a look of lust in his eyes. Lane had made me uncomfortable. But this man made my skin crawl from my body and hide in the woods.

A leather band bound my wrists and tethered me to a large tree. I drew my legs close to me and scrutinized the two men quietly. I had to figure out a way to survive until Torric could get me. There was no doubt in my mind that Torric would come for me. I just hoped he'd find me before it was too late.

Kree came over and stood above me for a long moment. His glare took my already frayed nerves and splintered them yet again. Malice dripped from every word as he said, "Ya'll be pullin' yer own weight as we go back ta the village."

I nodded quietly, nervous about him attacking me if he decided I was talking back.

He glowered at me as he untethered me, yanking me roughly to my feet. He started to load me with wood. Finally, I cried out, "I won't be able to keep up if you give me much more!"

He scowled at me and harrumphed. Tugging on the tether, he forced me to follow at a brutal pace. Soon, sweat was dripping down my back and the joys of that bath were far behind me. I wondered how Torric would find me. The thought that I might die before he could pierced my heart and caused tears to form in my eyes. I blinked them back and forged on. For hours they set a grueling pace. My legs felt like great weights, and each step was torture—but I couldn't stop, and I couldn't show weakness. If I did, who knew what they would do? Each step took me farther away from Torric and lessened the chances of him finding me. My heart iced over and I almost cried out at the thought that suddenly flooded my mind: What if they killed him before they found me?

No. I couldn't let myself think like that.

As the forest cleared, we came upon a village encased in a red wall. It struck me how much it looked like Vella, with the huge temple looming up from the center of the village. Jerking the tether, they headed toward the large red gate. If they dragged me inside, it lessened the chances of Torric being able to get me out. Dropping the wood, I started to struggle. Kree came over and backhanded me. Stars flashed before my eyes as I fell to the ground. He grabbed my arm roughly and shook me. "Stop strugglin', witch!"

"I can't," I cried. "I can't go in there! Please! Don't you have a guardhouse or something out here? I can't enter those red walls!"

Kree examined me for a long time. My eyes were wide with fright, genuine terror, which only helped my cause. I needed to stay outside this village to give Torric time to find me. Fortunately for me, whatever it was that Kree saw in my panicky eyes must have caused him to believe me because he nodded gruffly and stood up. "Tie the witch ta the post outside. We'll leave her 'ere until it's time."

"Time for what?" I whispered shakily.

Kree turned to me, and his vile grin tore the breath from my lungs. I had been terrified of the young man, but what I saw in Kree's eyes filled me with intense dread. "Why, for yer burning, witch."

"NO!" I screamed and struggled as they dragged me to the post and tied my tether to it. The younger man stood watch while Kree talked to the guards. Soon one of the guards replaced him. The young man's look as he left stilled my heart for a few moments. Knees buckling underneath me, I sank to my haunches and stared up at the guard. He scrutinized me with cold brown eyes that froze my blood as my heart leaped wildly to try to force the cold ice through my veins. Kree had talked me free of rape because of his superstition, but there was no telling what someone else might do.

When he finally turned his back to me, I went slack and stared at the ground in despair. Hours passed, the guards changed, and still no Torric. My heart ached. Either he couldn't find me or he was dead. I pleaded with any Spirit that would listen to keep him alive. At least if I couldn't see him again, the idea that he was still alive gave me comfort.

Some of the villagers left the security of the wall and came out to start building something. For a time, I watched as they cut and nailed the wood into a shape I didn't understand. At least, not at first. It was a small platform with a large stake in the center. My heart skittered to a halt as what they were building sunk in. They were preparing to burn me. Of course, they didn't have it ready in advance. They didn't know they were going to burn a witch. Icicles pierced my soul, and for a moment I couldn't even hear the pounding of hammers. Even my heart seemed to fall silent. When it started again, it pounded in my chest so wildly, I thought my rib cage would break. I was quivering with cold, and yet sweat poured out of me. I couldn't believe it. These people who didn't even know me really were going to kill me for being a witch.

"I'm a healer! I'm a healer, not a witch!"

"Shuddup, witch." The guard came over and smacked me across the face with such ferocity, I fell roughly to the ground and lay there in stunned silence.

When my mind finally cleared, I stared up at him with teary eyes. His gaze promised violence, but still, I begged, "Please. Please, I am a healer, not a witch!"

He leaned down and got right in my face. His foul breath washed over me, turning my stomach as his words froze my soul. "A healer is nothin' but a witch that hides what she is."

The shiver that rolled through me then took all of my strength. My teeth chattered as I shook. What was I going to do? There was no place for me to go. My death was before my eyes. It mocked me as they pieced it together board by board. Eventually, I started to shut down. My eyes blindly watched the villagers, and time passed without my realizing it. Too soon, it was dark, and my funeral pyre tormented me with its completion. A small crowd was gathering. I thought there would be more, but soon I noticed it was a large group of men—no women or children. I wondered what sort of life the women of this village had. Were they oppressed or did they just not want to watch a woman burn, witch or no?

The guards grabbed me roughly and hauled me to my feet. My tether cut, they tugged me up to the platform, tying me to the stake in the middle. Numbness gripped my bones, weakening me, taking the fight out of me. I stared unseeingly out at the crowd of men. Realizing these were my final moments, I tried to focus because this was the last sight I was going to see—a bunch of men with hate in their eyes.

Shaking my head, I turned from them and tried to remember the emerald of Torric's eyes instead. Warmth flooded my heart as I remembered how tender they could be. I smiled, recalling the rich, honeyed sound of his voice, the dark honey of his laugh. Closing my eyes, I soon remembered the cinnamon and woodsy scent of him. How he was so strong and powerful, but he had been so very gentle with me from the very beginning of our journey. I smiled at the memory of his kiss. I wished I had just one more of those.

The scent of smoke seized my memories from me, and a quiver rocked me until my knees were weak; the ropes around my body were all that held me up. I let my eyes slowly wander over the men. There were roughly fifteen of them, all of whom stared up at me with a gleeful hunger for my death. *What sort of man would want to watch a woman burn?* I wondered. Tears slipped down my cheeks. A sob cut through me.

At first, I thought I was hallucinating. Behind the men, I saw Torric, his eyes on me. And they were burning with rage. He raised his sword, and then he struck down the first man he came across with a savage, merciless blow. The flames started to rise as the others turned toward him. They were unarmed. For a moment, I thought Torric would hesitate because of it. The death of the first man didn't quench the ferocity I saw within him. I blinked and he was suddenly upon the men with a thirst for their blood.

He was like the wind, swinging his blade and hacking down every man in his path. Soon, they were running for their lives. Yet, he rushed to them, cutting them down as they fled. I thought perhaps some would escape, but Torric was faster, and soon all fifteen were dead or dying all around. For once, the need to heal did not overwhelm me. I just couldn't feel for those men who sought to kill me for no reason other than my hair.

"Torric!" He raced to me, heedless of the fierce flames, moving quickly onto the platform. Cutting me free, he slung me over his shoulder and jumped away from the platform and into a dead run. He raced for the forest, his arm gripping me tightly to him to keep me from bouncing off. Behind me, there were screams. They would come after us, I was sure of it. "We'll never escape!"

"Before I came to you, I freed their horses and chased them off. If we can get to our horses, we have a chance." He kept running, and I silently implored the Spirits to help us make it as I bounced on his shoulder. Behind us, I couldn't tell if they were coming after us or not.

I shuddered. Never before had I come so close to death. Tears flowed freely, and I sobbed uncontrollably as Torric violently rushed on. "Are you hurt?" His voice was raw with anger and concern.

"No, you got to me before the flames did."

We reached the horses, which he had tethered to a tree. He secured me on the saddle, swung up, and we were off, riding as hard as we could. I leaned back into him, absorbing his heat, his smell, and the safety of his arms. He kept rubbing my waist, as if he was reassuring himself that I was there, in his arms. We rode through the night and much of the next day. I slept on and off as we continued our mad dash.

Eventually, however, we stopped. He jumped off the horse and then set me down gently. Unburdening the horses, he then tied them with a decent lead. I watched him as he silently got me my grandmother's quilt and wrapped me up in it. The fact that he wasn't speaking cut me. "Please speak to me," I whispered huskily.

He froze before taking a few steps away. Then, he said softly, "I nearly lost you."

"Torric, I'm alive."

He turned and rushed to me, hauling me up into his arms, crushing my body against his. "I thought I'd never see you again!"

Then his mouth crashed down on mine as he kissed me hungrily, passionately, and for once, he didn't slow down. Soon I was on my back, on the quilt. His hands ran over my body, grasping me in places no one had touched before. I trembled and moaned in his arms, my heart dancing from his touch. With great effort, he stopped kissing me and rose up enough to gaze down at me. "Tell me to stop," he begged. "If you don't tell me to stop, I won't."

I smiled up at him and touched his cheek. "Don't stop."

Fire flashed in his eyes and his mouth descended on mine again. I could feel his hands on my clothing. He lifted me up enough so that he could pull my shirt up and off. He paused, his eyes an inferno as he gazed down at me. Fervor filled my veins, and I turned away nervously from the raw, sensual need in his eyes. He grabbed my chin and gently drew my gaze back to his. His eyes were penetrating as he stared down at me; I felt them pierce my soul. Growling, he said, "Don't look away. Don't shy from me."

My breath caught and I nodded wordlessly. His eyes roamed over my breasts hungrily. Leaning forward, he started to kiss me again with a gentler urgency as his hands ran over my chest. I gasped as he softly stroked my exposed breasts. When his thumbs brushed over my nipples, my back arched up and I shivered. In the time I had known him, I hadn't realized what it was I'd been craving, until he touched me like this.

As he kissed me, his hand ran down my side and grasped my hip. He yanked my hips to him, and I let out the softest little noise of delight as I realized the intensity of his desire. When he lifted his body from mine just a little, I let out an angry noise even though his lips remained on mine. Soon, I realized he was liberating me of my skirt. I squirmed in his arms, feeling a fire course through my veins and sink deep into my core. I yearned for his touch and feared what it meant. But that fear was not enough to make me ask him to stop. In fact, excitement was dancing along my skin.

When I was finally naked beneath him, his hands started to roam endlessly. From a cold place within me, I felt a fire, which ignited the heated passion already burning inside of me. All feelings of nervousness burned away at the intensifying ardor. My thoughts were consumed with him and being his. I leaned up and kissed him deeply, letting my tongue flicker into his mouth clumsily. When his tongue delved into my mouth, I suckled on it, and he moaned. I smiled as we kissed, reveling in my newfound power over him as his fingers brought me to life, my body writhing wildly under his command. Then, his hands made quick work of his pants. When he was free of them, he paused and gazed down at me while the fingers of one of his hands continued to stoke the inferno rising inside me. I whimpered as I looked up at him. He whispered one last time, "You're sure?"

I let out a small giggle. "You must have amazing resistance, because there's no way I could say no to you right now."

He frowned and his hand stopped its delicious torment. "Do you want to say no?"

I stared up at him. "I want to be yours, Torric of Glane. Yours and yours alone. Make me your woman."

He growled and lowered his lips to mine. When we finally joined, I made a little squeak. I wasn't surprised at the flash of pain, but I was thankful it was brief. But that little squeak caused him to pause. He leaned up and his eyes ran over my face with a tender smile as he waited for me to get used to him. When he seemed satisfied that I was ready, he started rocking against me — slowly at first, but the intensity grew with each thrust. My breath came in quick, uncontrolled gasps. Soon, all my senses were flooded with the need to be like this forever. All there was in this world was the two of us as one.

Need built within me, desire running like fire through my system. Pleasure coiled in my center, making me cry out. I didn't think that there could be anything better than what I was feeling at that moment — until suddenly, there was. I screamed out as the waves took me, and when they subsided, I found myself cradled in his arms. We rested there, our eyes locked. For the first time in my life, I felt complete. Truly complete.

Eventually, I drifted off in his arms. His heat surrounded me, his rich scent enveloped me. If I never woke up, it wouldn't have mattered, because a deep sense of peace filled me.

Chapter Seven

When I awoke, I was shivering and alone, the homey scent of oatmeal filling the air. For a moment, I wondered if it had really happened. But it had. My soul almost flew away from me as shyness took hold, and I burrowed into the quilt, my hand wrapping around my pendant. Toward the fire came a laugh. "I'd like to have had you wake in my arms our first morning, but I want us to get a move on today. We don't know if those villagers will pursue us, and I want to get some distance. I've made you breakfast, lass. Please come eat."

Sitting up, my eyes timidly turned his way and found his intense emerald gaze upon me. I smiled up at him and tore my eyes away. Everything that had happened in the night flooded through me. Glancing up at him again, I found him plating the food. Getting up, I moved to sit next to him, and he handed me breakfast. As I ate, I kept my eyes resolutely on the fire. I was far too embarrassed to look his way.

When I finished, his hand softly took my chin and turned my face to his. Tenderly, his thumb stroked my cheek. "Do you regret it?"

My eyes widened. "No! I could never regret that. Not…not with you."

Something relaxed in his eyes and he smiled. "Good. You just won't look at me, and I was getting worried."

"It's just…embarrassing." My voice pitched a little high.

He leaned over and kissed my brow softly. Fervently, he whispered, "Lass, don't be embarrassed. It was fantastic."

I laughed and burrowed into his chest to hide from his gaze. Nuzzling my nose against him, I inhaled his intoxicating scent. He pulled me tightly to his chest and for a short while, we sat like that. My embarrassment left me, and only contentment remained as I felt the powerful, steady beat of his heart under my cheek. Then he reluctantly let me go. "I'm going to get the camp cleaned up. I want to get us out of here."

As he went about that, I went to my boxes because there was something I needed to make sure of. While I couldn't heal myself, I could sense if there were any changes to my body or anything wrong with me. Glancing back, I found Torric occupied. I slipped my hand over my belly and let my senses sink into me. Once before, I had been able to tell that a woman was pregnant, and she hadn't even missed her first cycle. So I searched myself, seeking that first spark of new life. There was nothing. For a moment, I didn't know how to feel. Being on the road while pregnant would be hard, so a part of me was grateful. Still…the thought of not having a piece of him was upsetting. My mother had warned me once that it was notoriously difficult to get a female healer pregnant because of the toll healing took on the body. Considering the trip we had ahead of us, I decided that was a good thing. Besides, once we got to Kingshold, there was the real possibility that Torric might end this.

The trouble was, if we were together intimately again, there was the risk of pregnancy no matter how small, and as long as I was on the road, I didn't think it was a good idea. What if I miscarried or had some other sort of complication? There was no telling what would happen, which left only one thing that I could do. Opening the box, I pulled out a jar containing phellon. Phellon was good for many things, not the least of which was preventing pregnancy. Pulling out a small piece, I started to chew on the bitter root.

"What are you doing?"

I closed up the box and turned to him with a smile. "Just a little something to help me. Are we ready?"

He nodded. "Just have to get the boxes up and your quilt put away."

I went and grabbed my quilt, folding it up before putting it back in the box. Inspecting the blue-gray fabric, I frowned with worry. Each day, it grew dingier, and it was in desperate need of a good washing. Probably some repairs as well. I hoped they wouldn't be beyond my skill when the time came.

Turning, I found Torric's eyes on me. I gasped at the desire I found in his stare. In three quick steps, the gap between us closed, and his lips were on mine. For a moment, we kissed eagerly, and then he pulled back with a frown. "What is that bitter flavor?"

"Phellon."

He frowned. "Why are you chewing that?"

"Phellon is good for a lot of things."

For a brief moment, I thought hurt flashed in his eyes. "I know what phellon is good for. Why are you taking it?"

I sighed softly. "You and I have a long way to travel. It would be a lot easier if I didn't get pregnant on the way."

He opened his mouth to say something, and I could see when he changed his mind. Spinning from me, I thought he was going to finish loading up the horses, but he suddenly stopped. "Would it be so bad…to have my child?'

Understanding dawned on me and I moved to him, curling up against to his back. "No. That would be amazing. But think about it. We have a long way to go. If I got pregnant, it could slow us down. Or it could be worse. What if there were complications? I can't heal myself."

He turned back to me and pulled me into his chest. His lips gently brushed my temple, and contentment warmed my body. When I finally met his eyes, I could see the warmth within his gaze, and I couldn't stop a smile from flirting with my lips.

When he spoke, his tone had relaxed into its usual, rich warmth. "That makes sense. I should have thought of that. When I realized what you were chewing, I just assumed. I'm sorry."

With that, my heart eased. I glanced up at him before saying, "Honestly, your reaction surprises me. The last thing a man usually wants is to find out the woman he is not married to is pregnant."

His hand caressed my cheek tenderly. "Right. Marriage. Zianya?"

"Yes?"

He stared down at me for a long moment, his eyes intense. Then he shook his head and turned to finish putting the boxes on the packhorse. Walking over to me, he swept me into his arms before he placed me on his horse and swung up behind me. Then we were off at a canter. I could feel his anxiety to put distance between us and the village in the stiffness of his arms and body.

We went on like that for the next five days, making great time toward the pass. We'd eat on the road, only stopping for brief breaks. We'd ride late into the night before we would find a campsite. After we'd eat, Torric would make love to me, and each time was better than the last as I became more comfortable with our intimacy. He'd wake me in the early dawn in his arms before we'd eat and move on.

The closer we got to the Pass of Winds, however, the more restless he became.

"What is it that's got you nervous?" I asked one evening.

He gazed up at me over our dinner. For a moment, I didn't think he'd answer me, but then he sighed. "Getting through the pass on my own was hard. I didn't have horses or you. There's a path that isn't guarded, but it's treacherous."

Amusement filled me. "You're worried I'll slow you down."

He chuckled. "No. I'm worried about you getting hurt. As I said, it's treacherous. Most places are barely wide enough for a horse."

I glanced over at the pack animal. Biting my bottom lip, I tried to contain my disappointment as I asked, "You want me to leave my things?"

There was a long pause. Finally, he said, "When we pack tomorrow, necessities come with us. We'll bring both horses and see how it goes."

"Can we cross in a day?"

He nodded. "That's the plan. We'll leave very early and get to the path at first light. We need to be as quiet as possible as we travel."

A frown twisted my lips as a thought struck me. "Don't the guards know about this path?"

"When I crossed, I didn't encounter any. They probably know about it, they just probably don't believe anyone is foolish enough to take it."

My eyebrows furrowed and my frown deepened. The more he talked about this path, the more fearful I became. "What of the winds?"

Softly, he stroked a lock of my hair and tucked it behind my ear. "Part of the reason why this path is so dangerous."

I barely slept that night. When I did, dreams of falling plagued me. I was awake early for once without Torric's help. We packed up, taking the food, a few of my jars, and my quilt onto the horse we shared. Once we were on our way, Torric's arms tightened around me and I took comfort in his strength.

We were on the path by first light. At first, it was a gentle incline upward with grass waving in mild winds. But the farther we got, the narrower — and rockier — it became. The winds picked up and battered against me. I clung to his arm, nervous. My eyes wandered over the area. The greenery was gone, and the path curved up along the side of the mountain. My eyes slid back to the pass. It was large, halved in the center by a wall. In the middle of the wall was a large red gate. As the wind whipped the few loose strands of my hair around, I laughed to myself as I realized they were trying to keep evil out. On the Renth side of the gate, there was a large contingent of guards camped all around. I feared their arrows if they noticed us on the path.

The farther up we climbed, the more the winds assaulted us. I was grateful to have my hair braided, although the few loose strands were irritating. Nestling back into Torric's warmth, I dared to peek at him and found his hair was a wild mess, and I suppressed a giggle. He glanced down at me and smiled a moment before fixing his gaze ahead. His brow furrowed as he concentrated on making sure the horses carefully picked their way along the path.

When we reached the top of the path, about three-quarters of the way up the mountain, I trembled as the path got truly narrow. Torric clutched me tightly to his chest, and I sank into his affectionate embrace. He slowed us down and let the horse pick its way, giving our packhorse plenty of lead to follow up behind us. His lips brushed my temple. "Shh, don't worry, lass. I have you, and I won't let you go. I'll never let you fall."

I closed my eyes, and I whispered to whatever Spirits that were listening to please keep us from going over the edge. Suddenly, there was a downward shift. I opened my eyes to find that we were now slowly making our way down a sharp incline. I let out a little noise and closed my eyes again.

"Are you unwell, Zianya?"

"I thought going up was bad. Going down is worse. The world is just dropping away before my eyes."

His body shook with his quiet laugh, and then he brushed his lips against the shell of my ear. I trembled softly, heat rushed through my body, easing my cold heart. I turned my face to him and he smiled at me before gently brushing my lips with his. His hand played softly against my breast, the tip of his finger circling my nipple in a lazy rhythm and distracting me. "I've got you."

A gasp escaped my lips. "I know."

The day wore on and we made our way down the mountain path. It seemed like we would make it with no trouble. I peeked down and behind us. The wall was there, painted in a dark red on the Glane side. My whole life had been there, in Renth, in the village of Vella. Yet, as much as I had wanted them to be my people, they were not my people. Not really. My father was of them, but I was not. If my parents had not been True Mates, it was possible that my mother might have never married. I might have never been born.

Thinking of my parents made me wonder how they knew that they were True Mates. Was it a feeling? Was it something you knew instantly? I wasn't sure. All I knew was that with each passing day, my heart tied itself to Torric. If once we completed our journey he left me, I knew I would be in great pain. I tried not to think of that outcome. I tried not to think about the future at all.

We came to a stop, and ahead of us was a man with black hair and brown eyes standing in the road. He was dressed in the red uniform of the guard, and his blade was drawn. Torric's hard body stiffened behind me. My heart fluttered a moment. There was only just enough room to get off the horse. The man's turbulent eyes flickered between the two of us.

"Stay here," Torric muttered as he slid down the side of the horse and moved to stand between the guard and me. His calm never broke as he asked, "Can I help you?"

Gruffly, the man asked, "What are you doing here?"

Torric kept his voice even. "My wife and I are traders. We wanted to expand our territory."

The man stood there, taking us in, his eyes lingering on my hair. He shook his head. "You're going to have to come with me to the base."

Torric's voice hardened. "I'm afraid we can't do that."

The guard sprang out with a thrust to Torric's abdomen. Torric spun, dodging the man's blade, grabbed his wrist, and then turned to elbow the man in the nose with the opposite arm. He shoved the man back and drew his own blade. When the man sprang forward again, this time Torric swung his blade, pushing the man's sword aside, and then he slashed down the guard's chest. He stumbled back, bleeding profusely. The desire to heal him flowed through me, but I gripped the horse's pommel with one hand and stroked his neck with the other, whispering to keep him calm. Behind me, the packhorse whinnied. The guard looked down the side of the mountain toward the guard post. He opened his mouth, but Torric was faster, sinking his blade into the man's chest. The man dropped like a stone, but the need to heal did not leave me.

Torric turned to me.

"Torric?"

He swayed. The gaping wound on his side bled profusely. My eyes enlarged at the injury. I hadn't even seen the strike. Slipping off the horse, I raced to him. Clutching him to me, I let my healing powers sink into him. Getting a sense of the wound, I knitted it together. Holding him to me, I flooded him with healing until darkness took me.

When I woke, my stomach growled and there was a dark, honey-rich laugh in my ear. "My little healer needs to eat again. I don't know what you did to me, but I feel better than I have in a long time. I'm more than healed."

My voice quivered. "When I saw you hurt, I just couldn't. Torric, I couldn't bear it if someone took you from me."

His body stiffened behind me and his arms flexed as he drew me into his warm chest. "I feel the same way, lass."

Some of the pan bread I'd been making at night suddenly appeared before me. It was stale, but I was starving. I ate it in his tender embrace. My eyes flickered around, and I noticed we were much lower on the mountain as the trees were all around us. Leaning back, I was still hungry, but well enough for now and gratified to be in his arms.

"When we stop, I'll hunt. We're starting to run low on supplies. But we're also only a day from the fort we have near the Renth border. We'll resupply there and then get going to Kingshold. We might have to stay there a few days, depending on what's going on when we arrive."

I yawned, and he soothingly rubbed my waist. Gently, he whispered, "Sleep, my lass. Sleep and I'll wake you when it's time to eat."

Chapter Eight

Fort Nyte rested atop a large hill of wheat fields. It was beautiful, with green walls, multicolored roofs, and large, ornate gates. Although, as I gazed upon it, I also noticed that it was imposing. There was a watchtower on each corner, with warriors roaming the ramparts. From this vantage point, I could see a large catapult. At the sight of that, I realized their need for defense. This close to the border, the aggressors could only be from Renth.

Torric's lips fluttered across my cheek in a gentle kiss and then he set us off at a trot toward Fort Nyte. As we approached, I found myself feeling swallowed up by its size. When we reached the gate with its intricate lion carving, Torric had a small exchange with a couple of guards before we entered with one as an escort. I looked around the courtyard and watched the men going about their business. The clang and clatter of swordplay rang through the air, telling me that somewhere, men were training. Taking a deep breath, I slipped into Torric's arms as he pulled me from the horse. A man in a black uniform with a small lion insignia over the left breast came over. He was tall, as tall as Torric, with large blue eyes and close-cropped blond hair. His shoulders were just a little wider than Torric's, and his stomach was a bit thicker.

"Tor! It's good to see you again. And who is…" His deep, booming voice cut off as he stared at my hair. Then he asked, awe making his tone quiet, "Is she what I think she is?"

"She is, Keig. This is Zianya. She's a healer. And she's…" Torric stopped and glanced down at me, seeming reluctant to continue.

Keig rushed over and yanked me into a huge bear hug as he let out a roaring laugh and twirled me around until I was dizzy. When he set me down, I stumbled a bit until Torric hauled me back to his side and slipped a possessive arm around me. Watching Keig for a moment, I decided that I liked him. I also wondered how long he and Torric had known each other.

"Zianya, do you think you're up to a healing?"

Concern immediately filled me. "What happened?"

Keig's eyes turned to Torric for a moment. When I looked up, he nodded to the man. I turned back to find Keig eying me quietly. Then he nodded to himself and said, "We were attacked a few days ago by some men from Renth. A couple of my men were outside the walls. They were gravely injured."

Torric spoke softly, "If they're too close to death, you can't ask this of her."

I knew he was worried about me. But if I could heal these people, I had to try. I smiled at Keig and said with more confidence than I felt, "Take me to them."

We made our way into the main structure, which was a large building, larger than anything I had ever been in or seen. Our temple would have filled only half of this building. With that thought, another came unbidden—there was a shocking lack of red in this place.

As my eyes roamed, Keig took me down a side hall and into a room designed for healing. Among the medics that were bustling around, seeming discouraged, were three prone men. The first man I approached, the need to heal swelled, but then I was drowning in the need to not touch him. Taking a deep, shaky breath, I turned to Torric. His eyes filled with immediate understanding, and he whisked me away. I knew he was afraid I'd overextend myself and die in the process. The truth was, when someone was beyond my healing abilities I felt it and could resist. Yet, the dread-filled green eyes trapped my gaze. He could not have been much older than I was, and this young man knew he was going to die.

The next man was just a little better off, enough so that I knew I could save him. I ran my eyes over him. He was probably in his midthirties, with light brown hair and bright blue eyes that were struggling to stay open. Fighting the urge to heal him immediately, I softly said, "I can save him. However, I want to see the other man first. Whoever is worse off, I'll heal him today. The other I will heal tomorrow."

Torric grabbed my arm and turned me toward him. Concern clouded his eyes. Smiling up at him, I stroked his arm gently and then turned to followed Keig to the last man. He was young, barely twenty, with brown hair and blue eyes. Looking at him, I could tell he was the brother of the other man. They had the same aquiline nose. I turned to Keig. "He'll live. I'll heal the other first. Tomorrow I'll tend to this man."

Gruffly, Torric said, "You've told me before that a major healing can take a few days before you can heal another."

Realizing I should not have been so free with information when we had ridden across Renth, my lips twisted before I took a deep breath. Putting my confidence into my eyes, I touched Torric's arm gently. "Get me some meat. I'll eat quickly and heal him."

My gaze fell on the second man, and Keig supplied, "Jort."

Smiling, I said "Jort. When I wake, feed me well, and I'll start healing his younger brother."

"How did you know Jern is his brother?" Keig asked quietly.

I smiled. "They look alike."

After several minutes, a servant arrived with some cold chicken, which I quickly devoured. After washing my hands in a nearby sink, I walked over to Jort and found a spot where I could gently touch him without causing pain. I let my power wash over him. The instant pain left him, the tension in his body eased, and my power slipped of out me and into his body to knit all of his wounds together. They were extensive, and I had never healed anyone so wounded, but I knew I could do it. If I couldn't have, I would have felt the need to not touch him. As the last of my energy flooded into my patient, I was suddenly light-headed. As I fell, I could feel Torric's warm arms embrace me.

When I woke, I was starving, and my head was pounding. I sat up, finding Torric by my side. He was up instantly. "Are you all right?"

"I need food and tayden tea. In either order."

Smiling, he gently kissed my cheek. "Good thing I know what that looks like now. Stay here."

As I waited, my eyes wandered around the room. It was large and had the feel of a high-ranking officer's room. I was on a large feather bed, but it was not ornate—rather, it was very utilitarian. The room itself was also unadorned with decorations but contained two bureaus, a table with two chairs, and a large bathing chamber. Immediately, I headed to it and was happy to find a tub, among other things. If Torric hadn't been due back soon, I would have taken a soak. Instead, I gave myself a quick wash.

When I came back into the bedroom, Torric had a large tray of food, which smelled delicious, and a pot of tea, which smelled bitter. I sat at the small table in the room and dug into the food. Sighing after a couple of mouthfuls settled into my stomach, I found Torric watching me with an amused expression before he sat across from me and poured a cup of tayden tea. I took a sip of the bitter brew and sighed again. When I was a child, I had often hated this tea, but over time, I'd learned to enjoy its bitter taste. "Thank you."

"You're ravenous today, my little healer."

I grinned, "And you're fussing over me, my brave warrior."

"You had me worried. You've been asleep for eighteen hours."

I stopped midbite on a chicken leg and blinked. "Eighteen?"

He nodded. "I didn't want to leave your side."

I smiled and a blush took my cheeks as I continued to devour my food. I'd never been so hungry. As I sipped my tea, I realized that this healing had taken more out of me than I thought it would. Torric seemed more relaxed, relieved. Worry still filled his eyes despite this. Finally, he said, "I told Keig that Jern will have to heal the regular way."

I paused again and frowned. "I'm going to heal him as soon as this headache leaves me."

"No."

"Torric. I don't know what it is we have, but I know this…" Biting my lip, I took a deep, calming breath. "I will never allow you to dictate whom I will and will not heal."

He let out a long and annoyed sigh. "That isn't what I was trying to do. You wore yourself down. You need to rest and heal yourself."

I kept my voice level but firm. "That isn't for you to decide."

His emerald eyes met mine. There was a hard glint in them, but I knew it was because he thought he had to protect me — even if it was from myself. I reached out and gently touched his hand. His other covered mine and softly stroked over the fragile bones, which lead to my fingers. We sat there quietly for a long time. When finally he spoke, his voice was firm but tender. "Zianya, I know you feel a need to heal, but if you wear yourself out, who will be there when people really need you?"

My heart swelled at the tenderness within him. His tenderness for me. He was far more than a simple warrior. Of that fact, I was certain. I met his gaze with a steady one. If he and I were to have any sort of future, he had to accept that he could not dictate whom

I healed or how often. "Do you know who the only person who fully understands my limits is?" I paused and searched his face as he waited for me to continue. "Me. If I could not heal a person, if it would kill me, I would know."

"How would you know?"

Even after everything he knew, his concern for my well-being clouded his understanding. I smiled. "I just know. Please accept that I'll never let you tell me not to heal."

He folded his arms and said with a furrowed brow, "I did before."

I laughed softly. "You mean when I felt the urge to heal an enemy? Did I fight you? Well, I did struggle a bit. Let me ask you this: did I tell you to let me go, that I must heal him?"

He watched me for a moment before he reluctantly admitted, "No, you didn't. You struggled a bit, but you were quiet."

"If I want you to stop me, I will simply not argue with you. I'll let you take me from the person. But it seems I'm a citizen of Glane now, and I'll not have you stop me from healing one of our warriors. I might need another bout of sleep, but I'm going to heal him today."

He scowled and looked aside. Even without that expression, I could tell this was eating at him, but this was important to me. If he was going to stop me from healing when I needed to, then we were going to have a problem. So I watched as an array of emotions ran across his face, the most prominent of which were anger, worry, and finally acceptance.

He studied me. "Fine. However, if you try to heal one of our enemies, I'm going to drag you away."

I laughed. "Fine. Unless I tell you otherwise."

He frowned. "For such a sweet lass, you can be so much trouble."

I grinned and went back to eating and drinking my tea. Afterward, I curled up on the bed for another hour until my headache was gone, and then I went to heal Jern.

When next I woke, Torric was sitting in a chair next to the bed. There was a sandwich nearby. He was watching it as if he were debating whether to eat it or not. With a grin, I reached out and snagged it. His eyes moved to mine, and I could see relief in them. "I was worried. I hoped you'd be awake soon."

I nibbled on the sandwich before asking, "How long was I out?"

"Only six hours."

I smiled. "See? I know my limits."

He scowled. "I still don't believe that."

"Believe what you want," I sung out.

He shook his head before saying, "Keig wants us to have dinner with him."

"When?"

"A few hours from now."

I pouted. "I don't have anything to wear."

"I'll go see what I can scrounge up."

I smiled brightly up at him. "Thank you."

For a long moment, he stared at me. In a flash, heat was coursing through my body. He took a step toward me, but then must have thought the better of it, choosing to turn and leave. For a moment, I sat there. Then I devoured the last of the sandwich.

Smiling, I got up, heading to the bathing chamber. As I searched the tub, I frowned, tilting my head as I noticed two faucets. I looked at them, dumbfounded, until I realized there was no place to put the wood to heat the water. The second faucet was for hot water. It was a wonder to me that Fort Nyte had such a thing. Grinning, I filled the tub partway and then slipped inside. I took the soap and got myself as clean as possible before I drained the tub and filled it again.

I sank into the water, let the heat soak into my bones, and closed my eyes. A bath where I did not have to heat my own water was such a luxury. I started singing to myself the song about the warrior and his woman. It had become our song, although I'd never admit it to anyone. Suddenly, Torric's voice joined mine. I opened my eyes to find him in the open doorway, a passionate gaze running over my nude body as he sang.

When he finished, a smiled flirted with my lips. "Interrupting my bath?"

An inferno of desire raged in his eyes and my thighs tingled. "Looking at you in that water makes me want to."

I laughed to try to ignore my response to his gaze. "Go on, now. I'll finish getting cleaned up and then dressed."

Mischief twinkled in his eyes. "Do you have to get dressed so soon?"

I growled, "Yes! I'm still hungry."

He chuckled. "I'm getting us a second pack animal just for food for you."

I let out another laugh before I sank under the water and scrubbed my hair one more time to rinse it thoroughly before I stood up. My eyes met Torric's, and he slid his emerald gaze slowly down my body, lingering on a few areas, lust simmering in his eyes. I blushed from embarrassment, but watched him as he let his eyes lazily peruse my body until they met mine. Delight shined in his eyes. "Look at you, getting less shy each time I see you." His smile widened. "But I still love that blush. Are you sure you want to hurry and get dressed?"

"Yes!" I cried as I stumbled out of the tub and nearly fell. He caught me in his arms and drew my body to meld against his. Gently, he kissed my brow. His hand, however, had a different idea as it slid down my bottom and dragged me close to him, kneading the back of my upper thigh. The power of his kiss turned into a fury of desire. I trembled in his arms and yielded to his lips. The perfection of the moment ignited my heart and my core.

For a long while, we kissed like that, his hands roaming my back and bottom, squeezing me and making me tremble. Then he lifted his lips from mine and said, "If you don't get dressed soon, I'll be taking you to that bed now."

Blushing brightly and breathing heavily, I dragged myself away and headed into the bedroom. He had procured two long skirts and two loose tops for me to wear as well as a wide, black leather belt. One skirt was a rich, reddish- brown, and the other a dark hunter green, and they seemed to be the perfect length for me. One of the tops was off-white and the other was a dark green. I thought they'd do nicely. Wrapped up in a sheet, I wove my hair atop my head. Once secure, I dressed in the dark green top and the reddish-brown skirt, deciding to forgo the belt. When I finally finished with arranging my clothes, arms wrapped around me from behind as his hot, solid chest pressed against my back. His lips were on my neck, and I shivered just as my stomach growled loudly. Torric let out a loud laugh. "I have to feed my little healer. Again."

I elbowed him playfully, and we left to go to Keig's dining area. The halls were long and wide. The ceilings were high and held up by huge, dark-stained oak beams. The walls were reddish-brown stones, and the floors were polished oak. Now that I wasn't so intensely concentrating on healing, it afforded me the opportunity to really look and realize I truly liked it here. It may have been a military fort, but it was warmer than all the homes of Vella.

The dining room, which I assumed was an officer's dining room, was a simple, large space much like the halls only full of six dark-stained oak tables. The room was empty except for Keig, and I was grateful for that. I wasn't up for a lot of the gawking my red hair often evoked.

He smiled affectionately at me and held out a seat, which I gratefully took. When he went to sit beside me, Torric grabbed the chair and growled at him. I laughed under my breath, but a glance at Keig told me he was shocked at Torric's behavior.

So I chimed in, "He's just a little protective. Since we've been together, I've brought him nothing but trouble."

"Oh, is that all?" But Keig's tone told me he didn't believe it as he took a seat across from me. His eyes flickered between Torric and me. Then they focused on the pendant around my neck. "Is that some sort of Renth religious symbol?"

My hand slipped to my neck. I'd become so used to it, it now felt a part of me. Not feeling the need to point out it was a protection charm, I said in a happy little voice, "It was a gift from Torric."

Keig's eyes went wide and cut to Torric. Something passed between them, but I didn't understand what it was. When he turned his gaze back to me, it was thoughtful. Then he smiled with a little wickedness in his eyes. "Seems my friend has been holding out on me."

"What do you mean?"

Torric let out another low growl as he glowered at Keig. When I turned back, Keig was smiling. "Just having a little fun with an old friend. Now how about some dinner?"

As he asked that, two women came in, carrying some platters…one of which contained a roast with some vegetables. After setting the platters down, one woman went about serving wine as the other cut up the roast and set a large portion in front of Keig. Next, she served Torric.

The slight blonde had an adoring smile for him. Torric, however, took his plate and put it in front of me.

She frowned and said, "My lord, that's too much for a woman to eat. Unless…" Her eyes roamed over me with a frown, and I suddenly felt…less.

Torric frowned at her. "A healer requires more. This woman has given part of her very life to heal two of our warriors, and you are going to look at her as if she's a glutton for eating heartily?"

The woman's eyes went wide and then she turned to me. "My apologies."

I smiled. "Not to worry. Most people don't understand the foibles of a healer. We'd like to keep it that way."

She nodded and got Torric's plate before the two women left. The blonde shot me an icy glance before leaving the room. That woman did not like me. In fact, her gaze reminded me of Senna's. But I had other things on my mind.

I turned to Torric, studying him for a moment before my lips twisted in amusement. "My lord?"

Keig laughed. "He didn't tell you?"

"No, he did not." Mischief colored my voice. "Please, enlighten me?"

Torric leaned in. "Please don't."

I grinned. "Please do."

"His sister is married to the king."

"That, I knew."

Keig leaned in conspiratorially. "Did you know his family is the largest landholder besides the king? He's a duke."

I looked over at Torric with a grin. "A duke, hmm? Maybe I should pursue you."

Keig laughed. However, I felt he was laughing at something that I just didn't know.

Torric shook his head and replied, "It's just a foolish title given to my family because we've always led the king's armies, and we happen to own a lot of land."

I chuckled a moment before I tore into my food. Letting out a sigh, I closed my eyes, chewing a few times, before I moaned, "This is delicious."

"So, tell me, Zianya, were there many healers in your family?"

With that, I told Keig my family's history. He listened with wide eyes, asking questions here and there. The truth of my family's origin was obvious to him. I had to face the truth that I was the only one who hadn't wanted to accept the foreignness of my blood.

After I finished talking, warmth infused Keig's voice as he said, "Welcome home, healer."

Chapter Nine

"So when were you going to tell me you're a duke?"

My teasing tone brought a frown to Torric's lips as we walked through the red-stone courtyard, where not one tuft of green peeked between the large, flat sandstones. Off to one side, I could hear the clanging of swords and grunts of men as they trained.

Torric was leading me to the ramparts so I could get a good view of the area. After the question, he remained silent. So I looked at him, my eyebrows knitting together in question at his sour expression. He let out a sharp exhale. "I wasn't planning on telling you."

"Why not?"

"Because it's a foolish title. I lead our king's armies, and I happen to own some land, so I inherited the title and the position from my father."

I shook with laughter. He sounded so irritated that I had found out. Glancing up at him, I saw him scowling down at me. This only made me laugh harder.

When we had first met, I never would have felt comfortable enough to laugh at his discomfort. Now, I knew I was always safe with him. Although, I had to admit to myself that I had felt that a lot longer than I knew it.

He reached out and pinched my cheek gently until I stopped laughing.

"You think that's funny?" His eyes twinkled as mild amusement replaced his annoyance.

"I just don't understand the secrecy. What were you afraid of?"

He let out a frustrated growl as we took the well-worn steps up to the ramparts. I suppressed a smile. Finally, he answered me. "All of the women I've known, the moment they found out who I was, they changed."

I stiffened a little and felt something I had never experienced before. Was that…jealousy? I glanced sideways at him and found him staring off into the distance as we approached the fieldstone wall that came to just below my shoulders. I leaned against it and stared up at him. After a few moments, I said, "*Women?*"

There must have been something in my voice, because he hugged me tightly as he chuckled softly, brushing his lips over my temple for a moment. He whispered in my ear, "Is that jealousy I detect, my little healer? Don't worry, lass; no one has ever touched my heart until you."

A flush filled my cheeks, and I turned away. He held me tightly to his chest and for a long time, I just enjoyed the scent that was uniquely him. A deep sense of contentment filled me. He was studying me with a smile slowly taking his features. "You don't look at me differently." It was a statement more than a question.

"No, I don't. You're still you." With a crooked smile, I shrugged. "But now, I just have to get used to the glares women are giving me."

"What do you mean?"

I shook with quiet laughter. If he didn't notice, I wasn't going to enlighten him.

Turning to look out across the land, I felt my heart tighten at the sight. It was rich, with a surrounding wheat field that I assumed was for keeping the fort fed. Beyond the fields of golden hues rolled brilliant, green hills. I could spot clusters of flowers out there, and I felt a desire to go hunting for plants.

Torric must have seen the expression in my eyes for he asked, "What is it?"

I smiled up at him. "I've not gone gathering for plants that I use in my practice in some time. Usually, until the growing season is completely over, I go twice per week. Those flowers out there call to me."

"Call to you?"

There was a touch of awe in his voice, so I quickly added, "Not literally. I know which plants do what from my mother's teaching. She learned from her mother and so forth. That quilt of mine has a carefully stitched representation of each beneficial plant. I really need to get that cleaned and then repair it."

"So you have other skills?" His teasing tone was low in my ear.

I chuckled. "I wouldn't have called it a skill, but yes, I can quilt. My grandmother taught me."

"We're going to stay here for several more days. Why don't you tend to that while we're here?"

A frown took me and I found myself curious. Before, he'd been so intent on getting me to Donner. "And what are you going to do?"

He turned away. I grabbed his thickly muscled arm to turn him back to me. My hand looked so tiny against him and the strength that lay within his hard, coiled muscles struck me. He was watching me and his amazing emerald eyes softened as his fingers caressed my cheek with such gentleness from those powerful, blunt fingers. Yet, I could see the war going on in those warm eyes. Part of him wanted to tell me what was going on, but the other feared my response.

Understanding dawned on me. "You're going to leave me here and go somewhere."

For a moment, he struggled for the words and then nodded. "I don't want to. But there's something going on near the border of Renth, and Keig needs to know what."

"Why can't he send someone else?" I grumbled.

His fingers were feather-light as they stroked the bone of my cheek. Leaning down, he kissed me gently before he replied, "Right now, he's a little undermanned. I'm going to scout and then give Donner my opinion about what to do here."

It would be the first time we'd been apart since we met, and I found myself loathing the idea. I kissed his neck softly all the way up to his ear, where I let out a breathy question, "Can I not entice you to stay?"

A growl rumbled against my neck. "I want to, but I can't."

Laughing, I pulled myself into his arms and said, "Well, I had to try."

He squeezed me to his side and looked out onto the fields. "How about before I leave, I take you gathering?"

"You don't have to, I usually do it alone."

"I don't want you alone out there." The tone of his voice tolerated no argument. He feared something would happen to me out there. Considering the men I'd healed and the one I could not, I realized it wasn't safe the way it was around Vella. Although even Vella had troubles, I knew the land well, and I knew where to hide to avoid bandits. Here, I didn't. So I nodded, and he relaxed instantly. "When do you want to go?"

My lips twisted into a little frown. "When do you have to leave?"

"Keig has a few things he wants to be done first, so the morning after tomorrow."

Worry tried to quicken my heart, but I pushed it down. Torric was a strong and powerful man who had come back from who knew how many missions before he had even met me. I couldn't let my feelings distract him. So I smiled up at him and said, "Then let's leave in the late morning tomorrow and spend a few hours."

We packed up a lunch, a blanket, and a few empty saddlebags and then rode out. Torric's warm arm held me in place. Without the packhorse, he was able to let loose into a wild gallop and let out a cry of delight. Our gallop took us beyond the wheat fields and deep into the rolling green hills. I leaned back into his chest and sighed. Being in his arms always made me feel complete, and this time was no different.

Sliding off the saddle, he reached up to grab me and pulled me into his broad chest. Before he released me, he gave me a quick kiss and a grin. I set off wandering the fields, snatching this and that. The sun was warm and filled me with a sense of peace. For a time, Torric simply watched me, a smile playing at his lips. Then he rose and joined in, bringing me a bunch of flowers. I started picking through them. "This is davaina. It's a poison."

He laughed at me. "It's also the flower a man gives to the woman he's courting."

I arched an eyebrow. "Courting? Is that what you call what you've been doing to me?"

He roughly brought me against to him, and I let a wicked smile dance across my lips. As I looked into his eyes, my smile left, and the seriousness of his gaze hit deep into my heart. With a throaty utter, he said, "I have been."

Cheeks red, I turned away, only to have my face tugged gently to turn back to him. His emerald eyes churned with emotions, and I was lost. When I awoke in his arms—apparently his prisoner—less than a month ago, I hadn't realized how much he would come to mean to me. Growing heat fanned that first spark into the fervent flames that danced erratically in my heart. I let my hand softly caress his cheek and a passionate kiss immediately rewarded me. We toppled onto the blanket he had spread out for lunch, his hands wildly roaming over my body. His hands ignited a fiery passion in me. Our kiss deepened and a moan ripped from my body, unbidden. I could feel him grin against my lips as he growled in return. When he started to work on my clothing, I tore my lips away, gasping out, "Wait, they'll see us."

He laughed down at me, "Do you think I chose this spot of the hill so that prying eyes could watch us?"

I glared up at him. "You were planning this?"

He softly bit the lobe of my ear and whispered, "Of course."

Soon I was lost again, and we made love with the soft winds caressing our bodies. Urgency colored his touch and his movements, and that caused worry to run through my bones despite the intensity of my response to him.

When he settled against me after, he tenderly stroked my face. I stared up into his eyes and, like him, spent the time memorizing every line, every plane of his face. Then my breath caught.

"What is it?" he asked me in a voice so full of tenderness.

"Your eyes."

A smile flickered in those beautiful emerald orbs. "What about them?"

"I just realized before we met, I had a dream about them. I couldn't see your face, just your eyes. I don't understand. I'm a healer, not a foreteller."

He said nothing for a long time, just tracing the bones of my cheeks and the line of my jaw with the softest touch. Finally, he uttered tenderly, "I don't know what to tell you. I don't know enough about healers to tell you what that means. I do know this, Zianya — I waited my whole life to meet you."

As my fingers tenderly caressed his cheek, my eyes searched his warm gaze. A feeling of completeness filled my heart, as if I had finally found the other half of my soul. Leaning down, he kissed me again, and molten fire ran though me. I trembled in his arms and hooked a leg around his hip. A spark flickered in his eyes before his lips crashed against mine, and we fervently made love once more.

After we had finished gathering some plants, had some lunch, and rode back to the fort, it was late afternoon. When we trotted inside the gates, I could see various men still practicing with their blades. It reminded me that while I was welcome here, there was danger all around, and Torric was going off to meet it. Alone.

I clutched his arm. "If anything happens, send for me. I'll heal you, no matter how terrible it is."

He nipped my ear, amusement in his voice as he said, "Hush, lass. I'll be fine."

I reached up to his cheek and stroked his face tenderly. "You better be."

He smiled. "Now, what are we going to do with all these plants we gathered?"

"I need a room with some hooks from the rafters so I can dry them. If we're going to be here for a while, I may as well make some things that the fort can use."

A half hour later, I had my own room with a large oak table. With all the hooks on the rafters, part of me wondered if a healer once used this very room. Torric had brought in my boxes so that I could go through what I had. I started by separating what we had gathered that day. He left for a meeting with Keig, and I sang to myself as I worked.

There was a tentative knock at the door. "Come in," I called out with a cheerful voice.

A girl just a few inches taller than me walked in slowly. Her hair was long and pale, and her eyes were a deep blue. Spots muddled her skin and yet, despite that, she was beautiful.

I smiled up at her. "Can I help you with something?"

She opened her mouth to speak, but then dropped her eyes. It was apparent that she was nervous from the tremble in her hands and the fear in her face. Putting down the flowers I was separating, I moved around the table and walked over to her. Gently, I took her hand. "Please, tell me."

"My face. I, well…I was wondering if you could heal my face."

I frowned. She was so timid, and I wondered how much of a teasing she had received because of her one little flaw. Girls could be especially cruel to one another.

Softly, I squeezed her hand and smiled. "I have a salve you can have that, with regular use, will keep your skin clear." I paused — once I was gone, who would make the salve? "Would you like to learn how to make it?"

"Learn?"

I nodded. "Yes. First, I should ask you — can you read and write?"

"I can."

"Good. And your name?"

"Kayla."

I grinned at her and she gave me a tentative little smile. "If I teach you, it won't be easy. You'll have to write down each formula I give you and repeat it to me because while we speak the same language, I can't write it. One more thing…do you know how to identify most plants?"

"My father was a farmer. I grew up learning a few things about herbs and plants."

"Excellent. First things first," I went through my box and pulled out the salve. "This is made from a couple of roots and several flowers. It's the first thing I will teach you to make."

For the next couple of hours, I spoke with Kayla, getting a feeling for what she knew. I was grateful that she actually understood the key differences between plants. I was also grateful Torric had packed an old book my grandmother had with drawings of the plants I used most in my work. I decided I would give the book to Kayla and let her write the names on each page so she could study it.

We separated each plant we had into bundles of like kind and tied them up to hang and dry. I was testing Kayla to see if she knew the name of each plant and how to write the name in her written tongue when there was a knock at the door. We looked up from the book we were studying. I could feel the girl tense beside me. I'd have to work on her self-esteem before I left. I doubted I'd be able to help her completely, but if I could set her on the right path and give her a new job with a purpose, she could possibly rise on her own.

"Come in!"

Torric's hulking frame strode in, a wicked gleam in his eyes as he sought my gaze. Kayla gasped beside me. Glancing at her, I saw her cheeks go deep red. I understood where she was coming from—I shared his bed, and the man still could still make me blush. Turning back to him, I lit up with a smile.

"How's my little healer doing?" His eyes roamed over me, appraising my body and drawing a fresh splash of red to my cheeks as he smiled at me.

"Well. Torric, this is Kayla. I'm teaching her to be an herbalist."

His smile broadened. "Good. Perhaps when we leave here, she can help."

When I faced Kayla, I found her blue eyes were wide as she stared at him with flushed cheeks.

I smiled brightly. "Yes, I'm sure she'll be able to."

She quickly turned her gaze to me as her cheeks turned an even deeper shade of red. I hadn't thought such a deep red was possible.

Touching her forearm gently, I smiled before nodding to her. With a deep breath, I started to put things away. She quickly helped me while Torric poked around the room.

"Got yourself all set up rather quickly, hmm?"

"Yes. I didn't realize it was so late until you knocked. I'm starving."

As my stomach growled, he grinned. "Good. Keig wants us to join him again."

"I can clean up in here," Kayla said.

Frowning, I replied, "I can't just leave you to this."

Her face lit up with an adorable grin. "Nonsense. You're spending all this time teaching me. As the student, this is the least I can do."

After expressing my appreciation, we left and headed to the dining area again. This time, there were several men at the various tables, and a couple of them sat at the table with Keig. One was tall, broad. He had a ruddy complexion with thinning hair. The other was short and slender, with long, ink-black locks and olive skin. They turned toward me, and I found myself shrinking back from them and into Torric's side. He squeezed me closer. Their eyes darted between the two of us and then stared at Torric a moment. They nodded, and the strange fear I had fled from me.

"Zianya, this is Vonn and Zeer. They do work for me," Keig said.

Sliding into the seat Torric held out for me before he joined me, I calmly said, "You mean they spy for you."

Both men turned their eyes on me. Once again, I felt that urge to shrink. Instead, I stared back at them levelly. For a time, they simply watched. Then the taller one laughed heartily. The shorter one smiled quietly.

"I like her, Torric," the larger man merrily barked, "she's strong."

I tilted my head. "Which one are you?"

The larger man said, "I'm Vonn, this is Zeer. You're right. We do a lot of Keig's spying."

My eyes flittered between the two of them. Then I smiled. "On my side of the border, no doubt. This is how you knew about that path, Torric?"

Torric nodded before adding. "It seems they're monitoring it now."

"Yes," Vonn said. "They've been making trips into our side of the border, too. They carried out that raid, but mostly it's just scouting."

"To what end?" I asked. "Renth has always maintained the border to—as the people on my side put it—*keep out evil*."

The men laughed, and Keig said, "They still think we're evil, hmm? I wonder what they thought of you."

I shrugged. "The people of my village only tolerated me because I could, and did, heal them. However, one of the villages tried to burn me for being a witch." I glanced over at Torric to see him glowering. I knew it still bothered him. "If Torric hadn't arrived when he did, I'd be ashes now."

"What did you do to have them want to burn you?" Vonn asked quietly.

"Have red hair," I said simply.

"That's the most ridiculous thing I've ever heard," Keig said.

I let my eyes rest on Torric again. Anger fought for dominance in his eyes. I could only assume that the discussion brought up a wave of heavy feelings. My hand tenderly ran over his arm and wove my fingers with his. He turned to me and softened. To remind him I was still alive, I squeezed his hand and let warmth lighten my face.

"They have ancient tales of flame-haired witches coming from the West and terrorizing them. Unfortunately, some people still cling to those ways. My great-grandmother had found and healed my great-grandfather. Because of that, he brought her home and made her his wife. When people sought to burn her for being a witch, he told them how she'd healed him and that she had come to Vella with the purpose of healing our people. I don't know whether you want to say *fortunately* or not, but not long after, the leader of our village fell deathly ill. My great-grandmother saved him. After that, people softened enough to decide not to burn us. But they never accepted us, either. People who wanted my wares used to come to the back door, wearing hoods to hide who they were."

Zeer rolled his eyes, and Vonn said, "Fools." I was beginning to wonder if Zeer ever spoke. When he still had not said a word by the end of the meal, I was convinced he didn't. I was curious as to why but never got the chance to ask Torric.

Chapter Ten

With Torric gone, I threw myself into training Kayla. Intelligence sparkled behind her blue eyes and for that, I was grateful. We spent our mornings gathering and sorting plants, and she never made a mistake as she separated them into bundles. Filling our afternoons by going over how to make the various potions, salves, lotions, and creams, I was delighted when she remembered the use of each one. However, the truth was, that I was hiding from the fact that I was restless and sleepless each night. Waking up with Torric warm at my side had become a part of me. Working hard helped me to forget that the bed was cold.

A few days later, the door opened, and a woman walked in. I smiled up at her. "Can I help you?"

"I came to speak to you about Kayla," the woman said. She was older, perhaps forty-five, with graying brown hair in a tightly wound bun. Her eyes were hard and deep brown. The deep scowl she wore didn't help a face that few would find attractive.

I knew that Keig was supposed to talk to the woman in charge of Kayla, and I suspected this was she.

"Of course. What would you like to discuss?"

"I would like you to release Kayla from working with you." It was strange how her wording indicated a request, but her tone was a demand.

"Why is that?" I kept my voice neutral. My dealing with people who hated me for no reason my whole life had trained me how to keep my calm.

She shook her head at me, and her slow, deliberate way of speaking seemed to indicate that I was a simpleton. Irritation radiated in her eyes at my apparent ignorance. "Kayla is a foolish girl. She'll never understand what she's doing. She's a good worker but not very bright."

I watched the woman for a long moment, and then I asked softly, "Other than the fact that she's a simple girl, do you have a reason why you don't want her to work with me?"

She scowled at me and her tone allowed for no argument. "She's simple and is better off in the kitchen, scrubbing dishes, where she can't hurt anyone. If you really need someone to work with, I can work with you."

I walked over to the woman and looked up at her with a smile. "What's your name?"

"Ahn."

Now that the heart of the matter had shown itself, it was time to stop this. And yet, despite the words which next came from me, I kept my voice low and calm, "Well, Ahn, here's the issue—you want this job. You think it will bring you prestige, and because of that, you want to have Kayla removed from working with me. But Kayla is exactly the type of person who should be doing this job. She's kind, sweet, and intelligent. She has a natural affinity for the work, and I'm certain once I have finished training her, she will have the perfect bedside manner. I'll tell you this, Ahn. I'm going to speak to Keig again. I'm going to explain to him how Kayla is no longer under your guidance because you will be unable to let go of her to do this work. She's going to be working in the healing hall from now on. When I leave, she's going to be helping the warriors of this fort."

Her eyes narrowed. "Who are you to come here and make such judgments?"

I raised my head, "I'm Zianya, the Healer. I've spent my whole life healing and helping people. And while I am sure what you do is valuable to this fort, you have no experience as a healer or an herbalist. I know, because I recently familiarized myself with all the staff at the hall in case there was another I should also train."

Her already cold gaze turned absolutely frigid. For a few moments longer, her frozen eyes watched me before she stormed out the door. Outside, I heard a commotion with another woman softly saying *sorry*. A moment later, Kayla walked in and stared at me with troubled eyes.

I sighed. "Did you hear all of that?"

"Y-yes. I'm sorry. I didn't mean to listen in."

Her cheeks turned a deep red and I smiled. "I meant what I said. You have a natural instinct for this."

"Are you really going to talk to Keig again?"

"I am. Why?"

She paused a moment before saying, "Because I'm sure Ahn's on her way there right now."

"Let her. You and I have work to do. When we break for lunch, I'll talk with Keig."

We left and headed out to the hills under the watchful eyes of a couple of guards, gathering what we needed as we went. Kayla was far more relaxed than I had seen in all our time together. I had a feeling Ahn simply didn't like Kayla. But I thought she was easy to get along with and was quick of mind. I watched as she gathered only the plants we needed for the day.

We made our way back, and when we got into the fort, I found Keig waiting near the door, Ahn right behind him with a cruel smile.

I gave Kayla a quick wink. "Get these prepared for me?"

She warily peeked at Ahn before she nodded and trotted off.

I walked over and smiled up at Keig. Glancing at Ahn, I noticed her sneer spreading as a dark gleam twinkled in her eyes. Ignoring her, I turned back to Keig. Quietly, I asked, "Can I help you?"

"Ahn told me that Kayla isn't up to working for you, and that she would—"

"That she would be a more appropriate choice?" I chewed my bottom lip for a moment before I evenly asked, "Keig, if there were an invasion, would you want me to tell you how to defend this fort?"

Behind him, Ahn lost her smirk as Keig looked at me thoughtfully. He replied, "I'd hope you'd be smart enough to stay out of it."

"Exactly. When it comes to the healing arts, I've trained my entire life, and there's one thing I know, and that's who would make a good herbalist. This woman wants to take a position that I'm not offering her, and she's willing to say or do anything to get it. Meanwhile, Kayla has a giving spirit and a desire to help for the sake of helping. She may not have the powers of a healer, but she has the true spirit of one. Not to mention she has a natural affinity for plants and potions. Did you know she was raised on a farm and has some training with plants?"

Ahn pushed around him and spit out, "You wouldn't even give me a chance."

"No. I wouldn't. Nor do I have to. The knowledge is mine to give or not give as I see fit. I choose who my student is and who is not." Serenely, I said, "And a mean bitch who wants to learn because she thinks it will give her a better position is not someone I want to train. I could tell the moment I spoke with you that you don't like Kayla. Anything that girl was given, you would want, and it has nothing to do with your skills or even hers. She's smart and understands what I'm teaching her. She is my chosen student."

Keig stared at me for a long time, his eyes assessing. Finally, he said, "Who am I to second-guess a well-trained healer? If she believes Kayla should be our herbalist, she must know what she's talking about."

Ahn bit out, "But that job should be mine! I've worked hard here for years. That little girl has only been here a few months."

I let my eyes meet Ahn's. It took a lot for me to not let the smile that flitted across my lips burst forth. Keig looked at her with a frown. Suddenly, Ahn realized she'd exposed herself. Fearful eyes flickered to Keig and then back to me. When she spoke, her voice shook just a little. "I need to get back to work."

And with that, she walked away.

My eyes met Keig's. For a moment, we just stared at one another. Then he shook as a laugh burst from him. His laugh was infectious, and soon I was laughing, too.

"So how often does she bring you into her troubles?"

His eyebrows shot up and humor lit his eyes. "She's been complaining about Kayla since she came here. She's complained about other girls as well."

"Were they pretty?"

He frowned. "As a matter of fact, they were."

I shrugged. "Some women can be petty about things like that. Ahn strikes me as someone bitter who likes to use her power against those whom she views as a threat."

His skepticism at my assertion was rather obvious. "How can you be sure? You barely know her."

"You're right, but I've met the type before. Where I was from, I dealt with many women who hated me for many reasons that I didn't understand. After she came to my workroom demanding that I choose her over Kayla, I let her know that I was going to talk to you. My reason was that I wanted to make sure that once I left, Kayla was able to stay in the healing hall as the herbalist. I'm going to give her all the training I can while I'm here. After I complete the mission Torric has for me, I intend to come back here and finish Kayla's training. It would be a terrible shame if I came back and found her slaving away in the kitchens having forgotten what I taught her. People in my line of work have to have a giving spirit. Ahn does not."

Keig responded, "I hear you. I'll keep her in this new position."

I nodded and turned to go. Before I moved he asked, "Can I talk to you later tonight?"

Turning, I smiled. "Sure."

He nodded, and I headed in to help Kayla finish sorting. Although she was working, she was fidgeting anxiously when I got to the room.

With delight sparkling in my voice, I said, "You're the new herbalist here. We need to get all these formulas and what they're for written down. You're going to have to work with the medic. Let him diagnose, you give him things that will help. When I come back, I'll finish training you."

She let out a little cry and hugged me tightly. I smiled and returned the gesture. I liked the girl. And now that her skin was clearing up, she stood a little straighter, had a little more confidence. She was going to need that.

The other thing that I was happy about was that I was right. She was intelligent. She was dedicated, and I found that she memorized recipes easily.

Later that night, after dinner, I met Keig in his office. One of the guards showed me in, but he wasn't there yet. While I waited, I poked around the office and found on the wall a huge map. As I studied it, I realized not only was it of Glane but all of Renth as well. There was also the part of the land that they were at war with. I shook my head. I still couldn't understand the written word of Glane.

"Moritzan. That's what you wanted to know, right?"

I turned and smiled. "Yes. Torric doesn't talk too much about it. I have a feeling he's trying not to scare me."

"Probably. Any thoughts?"

Walking over to a chair in front of his desk, I laughed. An eyebrow darted up as he stared at me. Finally, I said, "After my speech today, do you really think I have any thoughts about a war that I know nothing about?"

Sitting down behind his desk, he smiled at me before nodding. He replied, "Just testing."

He watched me for a long moment until I started fidgeting uncomfortably. I glanced over at the map and then back to him. It was interesting that when Torric stared at me, I felt excited. This just made me feel nervous because I felt like a bug under scrutiny. I wondered what it was he wanted. Finally, he grinned and grabbed a carafe and a couple of glasses. "Drink?"

I smiled. "No, thank you. I don't normally drink much."

He poured himself a drink and studied me as he sipped it.

I asked, "Is this when you ask me to tell you about the warriors of Renth?"

His eyebrows shot up. "Do you want to tell me about them?"

I laughed. "Well, I don't know anything. But if I did, honestly, I would feel like I was a terrible person to tell you."

"Why is that?"

I looked over at the map. My eyes wandered over what the Glaneans knew of the world, and it was so much vaster than I had ever known. My eyes traced my way back to where I knew Vella was. The details of the locations of our villages were impressive. Yet as I gazed at Vella on that map, it was so very small and insignificant. "Renth is my home. Even if it was a lousy one. If I ever go back, I'll not tell them one thing I know of Glane."

He tilted his head. "Why is that?"

"Because of everyone in this fort and because of Torric. Glane is his home. If I betrayed Glane, I'd be betraying him. Besides, in a way, I'm a citizen of Glane, too."

Taking another sip of his amber liquid, he stared at me until I was fidgeting once again. I felt he was building to something, but I didn't know what it was. Finally, he asked, "What do you think of Torric?"

My eyes went wide. I didn't know what I was expecting, but it wasn't that. He stared at me with a steady gaze and I let out a sigh. "That's a very personal question."

"I know. But Torric is an old friend, and I've seen a lot of women pursue him."

I inhaled sharply through my nose in displeasure. "Define *a lot of women*."

He laughed. "That looks like a bit of jealousy."

I turned aside. "That has nothing to do with you."

"As I said, a lot of women have pursued him. They all wanted his title, his power."

"I didn't even know he had any sort of title until I got here. When we first met, he was gravely injured and I healed him. I woke up having found myself kidnapped for my trouble."

He chuckled. "Is that how he got you?"

"Yes," — and now, I found I had to chuckle at the memory, too — "He didn't even give me a chance to say yes. I woke up in his arms on a horse."

"Yes," Keig laughed louder. "That sounds like Torric. So how did you two end up together?"

I squirmed uncomfortably. "What do you mean?"

"Are you telling me he's sharing a room with you to keep you from running?"

"Yes — well, no. You're making me feel like I'm having a talk about what happens between a man and a woman with my father. Don't get me wrong, I loved my father, but I had that talk with my mother. When I was fourteen. I didn't like it then, and I don't like it now."

Keig smiled and downed the last of his drink. "You're right. I'm stepping where I shouldn't. But Torric is like my younger brother and I need to know what you want with him."

Sighing, I leaned forward and stared right into his eyes. "All I want is him. I didn't know about the title when I started this with him, and now that I know, I don't care about the title still."

Keig nodded. "Well, then. He should be back tomorrow. I don't think we need to tell him this."

I rose from my chair and pursed my lips. The whole conversation had left me a little uneasy. "Honestly, I don't know if I will or won't tell him."

He frowned. "Well, I suppose that's your right. I just wouldn't want to upset him."

"But it's fine to upset me?"

He smirked. "You seem like a good woman. But I've seen plenty of good women become greedy when Torric is involved."

"Has he ever fallen for them?"

Keig paused. "No."

I smiled at him. "You should have more faith in your friend. I do."

With that, I left and made my way back to our quarters. I walked slow and steady. However, when I got to the room, I closed the door and glared at the wall. It took everything for me not to throw the glass pitcher from the table at it. Anger wouldn't get me anywhere. It was a useless emotion, and one I tried not to feel. So often, back in Vella, I had dealt with so many things that could upset me. It amazed me that in the short time I had been with Torric, I had grown accustomed to respect. I took a deep breath and reminded myself that Keig was just looking out for his friend.

After a long hot bath, I curled up into bed and fell asleep. I awoke to a caress across my belly. I stiffened and turned to find Torric having slipped into bed with me. I flipped onto my back to look up at him and then I kissed him softly, briefly. Letting my eyes roam his face, I found he was dirty…and was that blood? I opened my mouth to ask, but he covered my lips with his kiss. It was slow and warm, like his rich, honeyed laugh, and I sank into it. He pulled away and gently stroked my cheek.

"You're going to have to get us clean sheets in the morning," I told him with a smile. "You're a mess."

He snorted quietly. "I will."

"Want to talk about what happened?" I asked as my eyes searched his face.

"Not now. Right now, I just want to sleep curled up to your warm body. I've missed you while I was gone."

I kissed him tenderly and cuddled into his chest. "I missed you, too. It's only been five days, why does it feel like it was longer?"

He squeezed me to him, and I reveled in his warmth. Burrowing into his chest, I found it easier to relax than I had in days. His cinnamon and woodsy fragrance filled my senses, and my heart felt complete again. I nuzzled into him and he clutched me tightly. For the first time since he'd left, I fell into a deep and restful sleep.

Chapter Eleven

My eyes fluttered open and I reached for him. The bed was cold, and I frowned. Had I dreamed it? I leaned into his pillow and inhaled. It carried his scent, woodsy and cinnamon.

I heard a splashing in the bathing chamber. Grinning, I got out of bed and opened the door. He stood, there naked, with his back to me and I let my eyes peruse his body. His back was wide and well defined with corded muscles; his hips narrow, with a strong backside. Turning to me, he gave me a cocky smile.

"I got a bath going for us. I was just going to come get you," — his eyes roved over me in my chemise and twinkled with mischief — "unless you plan to bathe with me like that."

I stuck out my tongue at him and he laughed. Walking over to me, he untied the ribbon, which hovered just over my breasts. He stretched the fabric and pulled it slowly down my body, causing me to gasp as the cool air hit my skin and hardened my nipples. I leaned forward, reaching for him, but he scooped me up into his arms and got into the water, settling me before him. I leaned back into his chest and sighed in the hot water.

"Kayla came by earlier. She was a little worried because you weren't in your work area. I told her that you were taking the morning off and would see her in the afternoon. She told me she was going to gather plants alone."

I tilted my head to look up at him. "I missed all of that?"

He kissed my brow. "You were sleeping so sweetly."

"Honestly, I've not slept well without you."

His hand softly ran over my belly and I trembled. "Oh?" he whispered in my ear.

"I'm used to being close to you. It felt…lonely."

He pulled me tightly to him. "I know what you mean."

For a moment, I pondered telling him about Keig. Yet, as I thought about it, I decided it didn't matter. Keig was taking care of his friend. And if I were worried about what someone wanted from Torric, I may have done the same thing. So instead, I settled into the water and closed my eyes, just soaking in the heat and his closeness. After a little time, I asked, "So tell me about where you've been?"

He started to sing in my ear, and I sighed. I'd forgotten how much I loved his voice. When he sang, his voice was low, mellow, and full of rich warmth. I leaned back again and let the melody roll over me. When the song finished, I let out a soft breath I didn't realize I had been holding. I tilted my head back and kissed him softly, tenderly, and my heart swelled with so much feeling. I was lost.

When he pulled away, he smiled down at me. I turned back and tucked into his chest. One of his hands splayed across my belly and the other just gently ran his fingers up and down the length of my forearm. I always found strength when he held me, and this time was no different. I reveled in our closeness. In my heart, something yearned to come out, but I couldn't quite make it out yet.

After a time, I asked, "So, about your trip, what did you find out?"

He kissed my temple. "You don't want to hear about that."

"Yes, I…ah." My eyes went wide as his hand left my stomach and ran along my inner thigh. He then lifted my leg and set it on the edge of the tub. Gradually, he ran his fingers up the inside my thigh, tracing lazy circles as he did. Then his fingers swept into the center of me, starting a slow, aching torment. I arched back and let out a soft cry. Heat pooled low in my abdomen and his heartfelt laugh was deep and husky in my ear. The water splashed as my body twitched and quaked under his touch.

When at last I tossed my head back and let out a sharp squeak of release, his other arm wrapped around me and held me tight to him. Tenderly, he whispered, "I've missed that sound."

I flushed, and he laughed as he stood up, lifting me out of the tub and setting me on my feet on the gray-tiled floor. He stood before me, the water running down his body in rivulets that emphasized each corded abdominal muscle. Gasping, my eyes ran over the hard planes of his body, settling on the trail of hair just below his navel. A possessive feeling wove through my heart as he got out of the tub, grabbed a bath sheet, and proceeded to dry me with great care. He paid special attention to certain areas, and I was breathless when he scooped me up into his arms and brought me to bed. Before I even had time to think or beg, we were one. Rocking into me with wild abandon, he stared into my eyes, fire churning in his possessive emerald gaze.

After our joint release had thundered through us, I curled next to his side and tucked my head to rest on his chest. The truth of what I felt hit me hard—I loved him. But I didn't feel ready to tell him that. Glancing up at him, I felt nervous about what his feelings were for me. I knew he cared. I knew he wanted me. But when it came to love, I had no idea.

Eventually, he got up and started getting ready. I watched him pull on his leathers and tie them up. Taking a breath, I said, "Is there a reason why every time I ask you about your mission you distract me?"

He stopped and looked at me before pulling on a brown cotton jerkin. His eyes met mine and I could see that he was torn. Finally, he said, "I promised Keig I'd report to him first. I came to your bed because I needed you. But I should talk to him before I talk to you about this."

I laughed softly. "You know, that's all you had to say. I understand." He prowled over to me, pressing me onto my back before he kissed me on the brow and stood back up. I sat up, met his eyes, and grinned up at him. Before I could think about it, I said, "But the distraction was delightful."

He laughed and heat flushed through my cheeks. No one could make me as bold or, for that matter, as embarrassed as he could. I smiled up at him as he leaned back over me. His body filled my vision. With a waggle of his brows, he gently pushed me back onto the bed and then kissed me. His lips devoured mine. I reached up and wrapped my arms around his neck as my legs wrapped around his hips, and pulled his hard length to me. Then—there was a knock on the door, and he growled out an oath as disappointment danced through my blood.

Biting my lip to suppress a laugh, I noticed him adjusting himself while walking to the door. I couldn't see who was there, but it must have been someone sent from Keig because Torric suddenly said, "I'll come right along."

He closed the door and gazed at me. "I'll come by your workroom when I'm done." I pouted as cutely as I could manage and he laughed. "That isn't going to work."

"Oh well, it was worth a shot. Try to have a good afternoon."

"Don't worry, if it gets boring at any point, I'll just think about this morning." I laughed and rose from the bed. His eyes wandered over my naked body, desire igniting his emerald gaze. A flush went through every part of me as a tingle shot up my thighs.

He drawled, "Or maybe I'll just remember this."

With a wink, he left. Flopping back onto the bed, I bit my lip to hold back a groan. How had he gotten me so worked up with just a gaze? Shaking my head, I rose to get dressed in a dark green blouse and a reddish-brown skirt. After that, I headed out to my workroom.

When I arrived, I found Kayla hard at work, hanging bundles of herbs and flowers. One of the interesting things I found in Glane was that women would wear either a skirt or pants. Kayla had on a pair of black leather pants and a gray shirt. Back in Vella, if a woman wore pants, she had a bad reputation. I pondered getting a few pairs myself; my reputation in Vella no longer mattered.

"Afternoon, Kayla."

She turned her newly fresh face to me and then with red cheeks, her eyes flashed everywhere but at me as she started fidgeting. She suddenly nodded and returned to sorting. It took me a minute to realize she was mortified about knowing what Torric and I were up to that very morning. At least I wasn't the only shy one in Glane. Embarrassment washed over me, and I turned to start my work. Everyone else rather ignored the fact that Torric and I were having sex, even if they acknowledged we were together. Still, to suddenly have someone embarrassed caused me to feel that same discomfiture.

I took a deep breath and tried to sound nonchalant. "Kayla, I'm sorry about this morning."

She dropped the bunch she was hanging and scooted down the step stool to pick it up. Her little voice held a note of chagrin. "That's fine. Are you… well?"

I coughed at her deflection and smiled as I bunched some flowers. "I'm very well, actually."

She giggled, and I sighed. "Kayla, can you handle the fact that Torric and I are together?"

She choked out, "Yes. It's just he was…well, he was bleary-eyed and naked."

I froze for a second and then barked out a laugh. Looking over at her, I found her staring at me, her cheeks a deep red. Then, after a moment, she started laughing, too. Eventually, we settled down.

"I'll talk to him about that."

"Please do. I thought you were sick, and then he opened the door like that. I thought my heart stopped."

I sighed. "Every time I see him like that, my heart stops, too."

We laughed again and got down to work. After hanging the flowers and plants, we started grinding benna root for a salve that helped contusions to heal faster. When we had ground it into a fine powder, I dictated the recipe, which she meticulously wrote down. Once she repeated the recipe back to me and I was sure it was correct, I watched over her while she made the salve.

Her hands were steady and sure as she measured out each ingredient. Kayla's mixing technique was flawless, and when she finished, I knew that it would work perfectly.

As my eyes settled on her, my heart fluttered with our blossoming friendship. Softly, I said, "I want to stay here longer with you. However, when Torric says we must leave, I must leave. I promise you that I'll come back here and finish teaching you. You have a good understanding of the plants as well as how to mix them properly. The deeper understanding is learning to realize what a person needs. This will take time."

She lit up under my praise. I wondered how often she had received it in the past. But the truth was, she did a very good job. She was conscientious and took pride in her work. The few times I took her to the healing hall, she was also very gentle with the patients. But beyond all of that, I liked her. I had never had a female friend before, not a real one, anyway. I was beginning to feel she was my first one. Just as Torric had become my first male friend, and so much more.

Timidly, she stated, "I know it'll take time, but I really want to learn this."

I tried to hide the smile that flirted with my lips. "Then let's move on to the next formula."

We worked like that for a few more hours. I was just starting to feel hungry when there was a knock on the door, and Torric walked in.

Kayla's eyes went wide and started to roam over his body before she quickly turned to carefully avoid looking at him. I hid a smile and walked over to Torric. "Picking me up already?"

"It's dinnertime. What's been going on while I've been away? Have you been eating?"

I rolled my eyes and Kayla laughed. "Of course she eats. She's been making me eat more, too. She said that strength is important because you never know when a patient will need you."

Torric hauled me into his arms. "Well, she's right, of course."

I beamed up at him and then turned back to Kayla. "I think we're done for the day. If you have time, study the book. I'll try not to be late tomorrow."

"No promises," Torric rumbled. I laughed and Kayla blushed as she put things away. I went to help, but Torric drew me out instead and headed for the dining area.

"So I take it you still aren't telling me about your mission."

He frowned. "I was hoping you'd forgotten about that, lass."

I glanced up at him. "Tell me when we get to our room tonight."

"I will," he said, his voice tinged with frustration.

I folded my arms as it dawned on me. "Keig doesn't want me to know."

Torric paused a long time. Just as I started to think he wasn't going to confirm it, he softly said, "Yes."

"I don't want secrets between us. I—"

Gently he said in my ear, "Neither do I. But sometimes," —he stopped us just outside the door and pulled me to him, staring at me intently, as if he was trying to make me understand something more—"sometimes you have to wait for the right time to tell something."

My eyes searched his. There was something hidden there, something else he wanted to say. He opened his mouth and at that moment, Keig walked up.

"You two are just on time."

With a faint smile, I said, "We are."

When we walked in, I noticed Vonn's arm wrapped up in a splint. The need to heal swelled through me. Turning to Keig, I asked, "Why was I not called?"

"It's just a broken arm," Vonn said.

I turned to him. "And if you're attacked, you'd only have one arm to use."

I reached for him, but Torric slipped his arm around my waist and dragged me away from Vonn. I looked up at him and frowned. "I told you before not to—"

"I'm not telling you not to heal him. But I'd much rather you eat your dinner. You can heal him after, and I'll bring you to bed."

The three men snickered.

Immediately, Torric growled, "To sleep."

"Oh, I'm sure," Vonn quipped.

Taking a deep breath, I sat down. But the itch to heal Vonn wormed into me. I barely tasted my dinner because my eyes were on his arm. Several times, Torric tried to engage me in conversation, but I couldn't bring myself to look away from the broken arm. My body shook slightly as pain from resisting the healing wiggled through me. That was the hardest part—trying to keep Torric from noticing that it was hurting me not to heal. He had no idea that it caused me pain, and I wanted to keep it that way.

"Are you always like this?" Vonn asked.

I shook my head and pried my eyes off his arm. "What?"

"When someone is wounded, are you always like this?"

"Yes. I can't help myself. The need to heal fills me. There are only a couple of things that can deflect it."

"Oh? What?"

"If the person is too close to death, I feel an intense need not to touch him."

With great effort, I turned myself back to my meal. It was only then that I realized it was an excellently roasted turkey. There was even gravy on it, and I loved gravy. I took a bite and smiled. Now that I focused on my meal, it was very good.

"What are the other things?"

I swallowed and looked up. I found all of their eyes on me. There was really only one other thing. A flash of the past cut through me—my mother, teaching me a lesson I'd never forget. I didn't want to talk about it. Torric had said that sometimes things needed to wait for the right time, and I decided that this was one of those things.

Smoothly, I said, "It's forbidden. So I shouldn't speak of it."

Torric turned to me, and I stared back into his eyes. I knew he was curious, but after what we had just said, I knew he would not push me.

Keig, on the other hand, was very curious. He wasn't going to let my words stop him. "What things?" His demanding tone grated on my nerves.

"Keig," Torric's voice was hard with determination to put an end to the discussion, "a healer is entitled to her secrets."

My hand slipped to his under the table and I squeezed. His returned grip shot warmth through my arm and straight into my now rapidly beating heart.

I returned to eating and said breezily to Keig, "We healers have secrets because we've been hunted so terribly. Back in Renth, I'd be dead in any village other than Vella. You'll forgive me if I keep our forbidden histories to myself?"

He nodded, but I could tell he didn't like it. Yet, what choice did he have? Torric looked between Keig and me. I'm sure he sensed the tension. I knew Keig still didn't like the way I spoke about Ahn, even if he realized the truth of what I said. After all, he'd known her for a lot longer than he'd known me, despite her intentions. Plus, he was worried that I had some ulterior motive when it came to Torric. That last part irritated me.

"The compulsion to heal is immense. Although it's possible to resist with great effort, it still has ruled my whole life. But I like healing people. I like knowing that I can help them. I like waking up and knowing that I did some good. I'm sorry if you don't like me keeping secrets from you, Keig. But the truth is, I don't answer to you, and I don't feel as if I have to tell you everything. Just as I'm sure you're not telling me everything."

Torric laughed. "She's got you there, Keig." He studied his friend for a long moment, eyes narrowing. When he turned to me, I avoided his penetrating gaze. But when he spoke, I could hear the grin in his voice. "Let me guess—you questioned her while I was gone. Just as I asked you not to."

Keig frowned. "Maybe."

"No *maybe*. I know my woman. She's trying to be civil, but she feels she's got a bone to pick with you."

My eyes widened in surprise as they slid to Torric. In all our time together, all the times I chattered to him, I hadn't realized how much he was observing me. A blush heated my cheeks. I should've known. My own observation of him had shown a keen mind, one of the things that had begun the love for him that was now dwelling in my heart. "Torric, it's nothing."

"Nothing?"

I bit my lip a moment. Finally, I said, "Keig and I had a… misunderstanding. There's no reason to get upset about it."

I could feel Keig's eyes on me and so I met his gaze. Understanding must have dawned on him that I had not told Torric. He suddenly let out a chuckle. I returned his laugh with a smile. His eyes moved to Torric. "Your woman, huh?" Keig said and then glanced between the two of us expectantly. Once again, I felt that I was missing something.

Torric frowned and Keig rolled his eyes. Vonn and Zeer kept eating, carefully avoiding what was happening between Torric and Keig. Other than the topics of my healing and being Torric's woman, everyone was surprisingly silent. I wondered what it was that had happened on their mission.

However, it looked like I wasn't going to get any questions answered that night, because once the distraction of eating was gone, the need to heal Vonn once again overwhelmed me. Before

Torric could stop me, I reached over and touched him. I let the healing flow through me and knit his bones back together. The toll for knitting bones back together took a lot more out of me than knitting flesh, and because of that, I fell asleep faster.

As I passed out, I was confident that Torric wouldn't let my head hit my plate.

Chapter Twelve

The next morning, I awoke in Torric's arms. He slept heavily beside me, and for a time, I laid there, softly tracing his features. His cheekbones were prominent and his jaw strong. His lips were full, sensuous, and I smiled, remembering the tenderness they often showed me…not to mention the heat of passion. I knew for a certainty that I loved him. And because of that, I made a decision.

Rising quietly, I slipped into the bathing chamber to wash. Sinking into the tub, I stared out the window to watch the colors of dawn play across the sky in rich hues of dark purple, orange-red, and then, finally, sky blue. I was content here in this fort, but I knew I'd leave soon and face the king I had to heal. Torric cared for him, and his words made me believe that the king was an honorable man. Yet, everyone I knew would revile me for this act.

All my life, I had been taught that the people of Glane were savages. My experience told me otherwise. My experience also taught me that the people of my own village were cruel. Still, I found it hard to hate them. If I were to be honest, a part of me missed them.

Well, maybe not Senna.

"You didn't wake me."

I turned to find Torric standing naked in the door. My eyes slowly ran up his body, taking in every defined muscle. I'd never seen a man like him before. And even though the warriors of the fort were strong and powerfully built, none of them inspired the emotion and desire in me that this man did. His presence invoked a sense of safety that I had never known—along with intense fire and desire. I wondered briefly if this was how my mother felt when she met my father.

He walked over to me and gently caressed my face. His impassioned gaze lingered on my partially submerged body before roaming deliberately. Smiling up at his wandering eyes, I said, "You looked too peaceful to disturb."

"Care to share?"

I laughed. "Only if we genuinely bathe. I promised Kayla I'd work with her today, and I know that if you get your way, I'll be in bed all day."

He grinned wickedly. "Not just the bed. There's an interesting wall I wanted to show you."

Chuckling and trying to hide my blush, I adjusted myself to make room for him in the large tub. He slipped in and dragged me into his arms. Quietly, the two of us held close and soaked in the warmth of the water and each other. Gently, I let my fingers run over the hard planes of his chest. He tugged me closer and held me tighter. "About my mission…"

"I don't want to know."

I could feel the curiosity in him and turned to meet his questioning eyes. Smiling, I slid my body up to kiss the corner of his mouth gently. He turned his mouth to mine and deepened the kiss for a long moment before he drew away and stared down into my eyes.

"Want to tell me why?" he asked in a husky tone.

"Because you don't want me to know. And if it's something I can't live with, what will I do?" My voice hitched, "I don't want to be angry with you or fight with you over things I can't control. I—"

"It isn't what you think." His gentle voice cut me off.

I turned my eyes up to him—now I was curious, and all thoughts of letting it rest fled. "It isn't?"

Kissing my brow, he said, "No. There have always been border skirmishes between Renth and Glane. Always. They're once again doing so, but it isn't anything new. Renth doesn't have much of a standing army. You're all scattered with little villages here and there and very few warriors."

Frowning, I asked, "Then what has you so worried?"

He gently stroked back my hair. I could see in his eyes he didn't want to upset me. Leaning up, I kissed him softly before I asked, "Please?"

He let out a frustrated sigh. "I thought you weren't going to ask."

"I wasn't, but now that I know you're not going to war with Renth, I want to know."

His arm tightened around my waist and we rested in the tub as the water slowly cooled. When the water was, at last, a bit chilly, he rose, lifting me, and setting me on my feet. Wrapping myself in a bath sheet, I started to dry off. I kept myself quiet. When he didn't continue, I walked into the other room and went about getting dressed.

"You're angry."

"I don't know what I am. But there are things I've not shared with you, so I best get used to you not sharing everything with me. This being just another thing."

"Another thing?"

I froze. I hadn't meant to say that. I knew Torric was keeping something from me, but I wasn't ready to push him for answers. Quickly, I finished getting dressed. Turning to him, I smiled. "I'm hungry. Can we go get some breakfast?"

He stood there, still. I could see in his eyes that he wanted to pursue it. Then, thinking better of it, he turned to his own clothing and got dressed. I let my eyes wander over his body—strong, powerful, and without an ounce of excess weight. He dressed in his usual dark brown jerkin and pants. I smiled as the irritation vanished. When we had been on the road, he didn't have a shirt. I decided I missed that.

The next three days were full of my teaching Kayla. My evenings were lonely because Torric was busy with Keig, Vonn, and Zeer. When he'd arrive at our room, we'd make love, and he'd hold me through the night. He never spoke of what was going on, and I didn't press him. I didn't want him to ask me about the forbidden thing that healers could do.

Each day with Kayla, I felt more confident in my choice. She now had the most important recipes memorized, and when she'd mix them, she did an impeccable job. In addition, Ahn never bothered us again. I was content with my work and was happy to pass on what I knew. I realized I'd miss this place and those I had come to care for.

On the fourth day, Torric came to me just before lunch. He smiled at Kayla before he kissed me soundly. Eyes twinkling at him, I said, "What's going on?"

"I want to have lunch, just the two of us."

I grinned up at him and turned to Kayla. "I'll be back in an hour. Get yourself something to eat."

When I noticed the flash of red across her cheeks, I smothered a smile. Torric slipped his arm around me and led me back to our room, where I found a meal of roasted chicken and vegetables waiting for us.

I tilted my head and then turned my eyes up to him. "We're actually eating?"

He laughed and dragged me to him. His deep kisses stole my breath as he crushed my body to his for a long moment. After he left my lips delightfully bruised, he rested his brow on mine and looked into my eyes. His emerald gaze once again captivated me. Like mine, his eyes were green, but the color was so different. Before I met him, I never thought I would grow to love green eyes. Back in Vella, they made me feel so separate and alone.

"We're actually eating. I want to talk to you as well."

After he seated me at the small table in our room, he sat and we started in on the chicken. It was perfectly seasoned, and I got the urge to go to the kitchen and ask the cook what her secret was.

An affable silence filled the room as we ate, drinking a sweet wine with our meal. I didn't drink often, but this particular wine was delicious. When we finished, I cleared away the dishes and left the tray outside the door. I had learned from Torric the few times we ate in our room that the servants in the fort would take them away. When I returned to him, he pulled me to sit sidesaddle on his lap. He grinned at me and planted a soft kiss. Smiling back at him, I waited. I knew he wanted to talk to me. The question was, what did he want to say? For a time, however, he just held me close.

"What's going on?" I finally asked.

"We're leaving tomorrow."

A mix of emotions ran through me as I said, "That's good. The sooner we go, the sooner we get to Donner."

He stared at me for a long moment. "You don't want to leave."

"I'm enjoying training Kayla. I've never had anyone so eager to learn my craft before."

"I'll bring you back. I promise."

I nuzzled into his neck, inhaling his rich woodsy and cinnamon scent. I could live on it. In his arms, I felt at peace and a sense of belonging. I didn't think I had known what I was missing living in

Vella until Torric had come into my life and shown me warmth and tenderness. Even here, in this fort, most people treated me with dignity and respect. No one looked at me as if I was going to bring them harm. I could have been content to live here.

"So is that why we have to meet alone?"

He smiled. "We're leaving in the morning, and Vonn is coming with us."

I grinned at him. "That'll be fun." And then the meaning of his words sunk in, and my voice sank. "And we'll never be alone."

I let out a long sigh and he hugged me to him. "At least with two of us, it'll be easier to keep you safe."

"Why is he coming?"

"He needs to report to Donner."

"And we're leaving first thing in the morning?"

His fingers ran feather-light through my hair. "Before dawn."

"Which means we have to go to sleep early," I said with a pout. He laughed and kissed it.

For a moment, I hesitated. Then I deliberately stood. Staring down at him as he gazed up at me, I could see the raw want in his eyes. My skin flushed; I felt shy, and yet, so at ease with him. I touched his face gently and smiled. Leaning forward, I kissed his brow and then I hitched up my skirt to straddle him. His eyes brightened in surprise. Each time we made love, he had initiated it. This time, I decided I would show him how I felt. This time, I would be in control.

He leaned back, studying me curiously. I ran my hand down his cheek and his eyes warmed. When he reached for me, I grabbed his wrists and set his hands on my waist. Slipping my arms around his neck, I pressed my lips to his. My kiss was soft, tender, and full of need. He responded with his own. I pulled myself closer to him and slowly ground my hips against his. He gasped, and I smiled in delight that I could elicit such a response from him. Deepening our kiss, I let my tongue dance along his as I slowly teased him with my body. His hand rose to caress my breasts, but I drew back and smiled down at him. Returning his hands to my waist, I slid my body along his, teasing him as I nipped at his neck. His fiery voice, laced with amusement, caressed my ear. "You're quite the vixen today. What's gotten into you?"

My answer was a frenzied kiss, letting my hands run over his chest. I grasped the hem of his jerkin and broke the kiss long enough to wrench it off him. I opened my eyes as we kissed and for a moment, his gaze met mine before I started kissing down his throat. I let my tongue trail down the column of his neck as my hands ran down over the hard muscles of his chest and then to his abdomen. When my hands came to the laces of pants, there a sudden hitch in his breath. My eyes met his as my hands worked to free him. He grinned at my boldness, but I could feel my cheeks heating. It was exciting and awkward as I gently caressed the length of him, and his breath became ragged. Slowly, I ran my hands up his strong arms.

Before I had met Torric, I had never known a man's touch. and now, I was initiating a carnal act with a man that I loved. I kissed him, letting my love flow through it. His response sped my heart into a wild frenzy as his hands on my waist clutched me. His tongue caressed mine and drove me wild.

Biting my bottom lip, I shyly let my hands caress him again, and he quaked a moment. Our eyes met and he watched me with great interest. Intense desire filled me. The need to be one with him overwhelmed me and turned my hesitation to dust. With a swift thrust, we joined. A cry of delight tore from my lips. His emerald eyes were on fire as his hands slipped to my bottom and held tightly to me as I ground against him, gasping out in delight.

Excitement filled me, and I stared into his eyes as we made love. He grinned at me, one hand remaining wrapped around my hips as the other grasped my hair and held me in place with my head tilted back so he could scrape his teeth over my neck. I whimpered out his name, and his answering cry caused an intense blaze through me. My body started to twitch of its own accord, and I gasped rapidly before I went off for him. When his body quaked with his release, he roared my name, and I collapsed onto him. He drew me closer, his hand softly playing with my hair.

I said with a little voice, "I supposed since we couldn't be together for a while, I just…well…"

He laughed. "I enjoyed your boldness. And I like when you get shy, too." He inhaled along my neck before he bit softly. "And I can never get enough of you."

Despite myself, I pouted. "It's going to be strange having someone with us."

"I know. But Vonn needs to see Donner, and I want the extra protection for you."

"What's going on that makes you so worried about that?"

He lifted me and dragged me into the bed to curl up against my back. I snuggled back into his arms, reveling in the heat of his skin and the scent of his body. As his rough fingers gently caressed my stomach, I relaxed in his arms. I nearly started to drift. "What are you worried about?" I forced my eyes open as I spoke.

He laughed softly. "Well, I thought I'd be able to sway you."

I turned in his arms to face him and softly traced his jaw with my fingertips. "Please tell me."

"There have been reports of Moritzan spies in the land. Some of them are entering villages and hunting for something."

I studied his face for a long moment. I bit my bottom lip a minute before asking, "Something or someone?"

He frowned, and for a moment, I didn't think he'd speak until he finally said, "They've been asking about healers."

Things clicked into place. "You're worried they'll find me."

He growled, "You're safe here in the fort, but once we leave, if anyone sees you…"

I chewed my lip for a moment and thought about it. "I could dye my hair with telkroot or something. It wouldn't last forever, but it should get us by."

He took one of my locks and curled it around his finger. "I'll miss these lovely flames."

I laughed. "Think of it as having another woman for a while."

"Why would I want another woman when I have you?" His tone was so serious, my breath hitched, and I stared up at him with wide eyes. He grinned down at me and brushed his lips against mine.

I didn't know if he loved me. I thought he might, but he never said it. The fear that he'd grow bored with me one day tried to burrow into my heart. Taking a deep breath, I decided to bury that fear and wait to see what the future held for us.

"Then remember it's me under that dye."

He tugged me closer, his hand grasping my bottom tightly. "Rest here."

"I'm supposed to help Kayla this afternoon."

He pressed his lips to mine and held me in his arms, his kiss growing more ardent with each slant of his lips. He growled, "Rest here."

"For now," I said in a little voice. He grinned and kissed me again.

I never did see Kayla that afternoon.

Chapter Thirteen

With the decision to dye my hair, we decided to leave later in the morning. I was happy about that because I had wanted to take the time to say good-bye to Kayla. I knew I'd see her again, but I wasn't sure how long until I returned to the fort. I had trained her as best as I could, now it would be up to her to be strong and continue. At least I could arm her with the book we had worked on together.

Kayla helped to dye my hair, and when we were finished and I had braided it, I studied myself in the mirror. Fortunately, my eyebrows had always been darker, closer to deep auburn. The dark brown hair, however, seemed odd to me. I knew it would slowly fade over the course of two or three weeks, so I was bringing some telkroot to dye my hair again should the need arise. Tilting my head to the side, I frowned. My skin was far too pale.

"I like it."

Turning to find Kayla watching me, I smirked. "I don't. But it will get us to Kingshold."

She folded her arms, her eyes roving over my face and hair. Then she nodded in approval and smiled. "I do like it. It's different. I wonder if your man will like it."

Grinning, I turned to her. "I don't know." As I looked into her eyes, they suddenly glittered with unshed moisture. Walking over, I drew her into a tender embrace and tried to fight my own tears. I squeezed her tightly and kissed her cheek gently. "There now, you'll do well."

"But I'll miss you," she said with a small voice as I drew away.

"And I'll come back. We'll work more and I'll help you so you can start your own herbalist shop here."

"That isn't why I'll miss you," she said as her voice broke.

I turned to study the hanging plants to hide the tears that were threatening to spill all over my cheeks and said, "I know. And I'll miss you, too."

Turning back to her, I found her smiling, her cheeks wet. Giving her another embrace, I studied her eyes and nodded before I headed to the door, where I paused and turned back to her. "I expect this place to be filled with potions, lotions, salves, and creams when I return. Not to mention many teas. And don't let Ahn get under your skin—she she can't say anything anymore."

She grinned. "I won't."

I nodded because I couldn't say the word good-bye and headed to the courtyard, where I was supposed to meet with Torric. He wasn't there yet, but Vonn was.

He walked over and his eyes ran over me. I wasn't uncomfortable the way I felt when Lane would look at me. Vonn had an obvious affection for me, but it wasn't anything that was off-putting.

I beamed at him. "Well? What do you think?"

Grinning, he grabbed a loose lock of my hair and gave it a soft tug. "I like it."

"I don't," a voice grumbled behind me. I turned to find Torric glaring at Vonn, who moved away. When Torric came close, he stroked my cheek and gazed into my eyes. "My woman's beautiful hair, hidden under this dark dye."

I laughed. "Don't worry. It'll wear off soon enough. Depending on how long it'll take, we may have to dye it again. I have some for the trip."

He frowned. "I still don't like it. You don't look like you." He leaned forward and smelled my hair, which drew a laugh out of me, not to mention Vonn. "You don't smell like you, either."

I leaned up and kissed his jaw tenderly. "It'll wear off, I assure you." I met his emerald eyes and smiled. He stared down at me, tenderly stroking my face and I could see the worry in his gaze. I stroked his cheek and tilted my head. "You're worried about me."

"Of course I am. Glane is more dangerous now than ever."

"That's why I dyed my hair. As long as we keep me away from injured people, it shouldn't be a problem."

He frowned. "If we do find any wounded people, you're not helping them."

I rolled my eyes. "You don't dictate whom I heal."

"If it means your safety, you won't heal anyone." His voice was forceful, and for once, when he turned to me, his gaze was hard. Most would shrink from those eyes — and most would be right to do so.

But I knew that I was safe with him, so instead, I shook my head and walked toward the horses. In a small show of defiance, I said, "Who am I riding with?"

"With me," Vonn said with a wicked gleam in his eyes.

Suppressing a grin, I turned to him and his horse. Suddenly, an arm came around my waist and Torric snarled, "She rides with me, Vonn."

I laughed as he hauled me over to his horse and gently set me on the saddle. After, he swung up behind me, wrapped an arm around my waist, and drew me into the warmth of his chest. I could still hear Vonn laughing. A blush heated my cheeks and I peeked up at him. I found him looking down at me, and then he kissed me between the eyes. "You like to be trouble, don't you?"

I stifled the need to smile as we rode out.

Glancing around, I noticed we had three pack animals with us. One of them carried my grandmother's wooden boxes. This time I only took what I thought we'd need. Torric had packed many things that were more for beauty than for healing. We had supplies to last us for the trip and my grandmother's quilt, which I had cleaned and repaired while at the fort. I had needed to do something when I was sleepless.

As we left the safety of the black walls, I turned to look back. I was going to miss it and the people I had come to know.

Torric's strong arm embraced me tightly to him and I found that he was watching me, his eyes unreadable.   Finally, he asked, "What are you thinking?"

My eyes trailed along the road ahead and I whispered, "I'm just going to miss that place."

"We'll come back, I promise," he said, his voice rough in my ear. Then he grumbled, "You don't smell right."

I laughed. "You'll get used to it."

"Are you two going to be like this the entire time?" Vonn asked, his voice trembling with barely held-back mirth.

"I don't know," I said. "He's rather upset about how I smell."

"He's touchy. He's never been one to share his playthings. Doesn't like changes, either."

My eyes widened, but before I could speak, Torric growled, "She's not my plaything."

Vonn snickered. "No, my old friend. She definitely is not your plaything."

"Vonn."

"Hey, I'm not saying anything."

My eyes slid over to Vonn and I found him studying us with an amused expression. I glanced back up to Torric, but his face was unreadable. I didn't know what it was, but he was holding something back. I let my eyes slip over to Vonn. He knew. I let out a soft breath and shook my head. Torric would keep me safe. I had to accept that when it was time for me to know, he'd tell me.

Torric and Vonn set a swift pace. When we started, it was late morning; by late afternoon, my stomach was growling. When it got loud enough that Torric chuckled, he reached into a saddlebag, and pulled out some wheat bread and handed it to me. Tearing into it, I immediately let out a sigh of contentment.

Torric nipped my ear. Keeping my voice low, I asked, "You hungry, too?"

"I don't have a healer's appetite. I'm fine."

As I ate, I considered our surroundings. Green was as far as the eyes could see and it was loaded with spectacular spots of late summer flowers. However, there were no mountains around us, and up ahead, the area was vast and broken only by intermittent forests. It was so different from the valley I had grown up in, nestled in the mountains. I felt so small in the wide-open spaces of Glane. But the land had a peaceful quality to it. There were flowers everywhere, some that I didn't recognize immediately. But, as I looked at them, I realized they were all there on my grandmother's quilt. I smiled and wondered what my great-grandmother would think of me coming here to her home.

When evening came, Torric brought us to a lake to camp. While the two men set it up, I headed out to an isolated spot to bathe. I had just slipped under the water when hands snaked around me. Fear crawled through me, and I kicked to get away. We broke through the lake's surface, and I turned to find myself in Torric's arms. Immediately, I relaxed. Then I thought about Vonn, and my lips twisted as I asked, "What are you doing here?"

"The last time I let you wander off to bathe alone, men took you from me. I wasn't happy with that."

Remembering his face when he attacked those villagers set on burning me, I found the idea that he wasn't happy to be an enormous understatement. His arms held me close, and I searched his face. He was worried. Leaning up, I kissed him tenderly. His hand slid over my bottom, creeping to the back of my inner thigh and stroking softly as he deepened the kiss.

Gently, I pulled away. "I'm fine. You and Vonn are with me."

"I let you bathe alone before because I didn't want to scare you. Instead, I should've told you that I'd wait for you on the shore. I should've made you understand that I'd not have touched you without your permission."

I laughed. "Yes, but you would have seen me naked."

"I see you naked now," he said with a roguish grin.

I snickered. "Yes, well, since that night, many things have changed." I kissed his cheek gently and his hand slid over my breast, fingers brushing over my nipple. As he gave a soft tug, I gasped out. "Hey! Vonn isn't far from here."

His teeth nipped along the side of my neck. I shuddered as he whispered, "He knows not to bother us."

"No. I can't. Not with him right there."

His head tilted back and he let out a hearty laugh. When his emerald eyes met mine, they were full of mischief. He kissed my temple and my jaw and whispered in my ear, "You people from Renth are so foolish."

"Yes, well, back at home, I would now have a very bad reputation."

His hand snaked over my backside and brought my hips to his as we floated in the water. "Those fools had no idea what an incredible woman they had."

Giggling in embarrassment, I pushed off him to swim out into the lake. The cool water felt like silk against my warm skin. Soon, it would be too cold to take long swims like this.

As I swam, Torric kept pace with me. I'm sure he was moving slowly for me. I turned my eyes to him with a coy grin. Splashing water into his face, I swam backward. He laughed and splashed me right back. I dove and swam quickly, but I knew I couldn't outpace him. He dragged me into his arms, and we rose to catch our breath. As I stared up at him, my heart swelled and felt so full I thought it might burst. We kissed slowly and leisurely, my legs around his waist as he propelled us at a gentle pace toward the shore. When we finally reached it, he carried me out as I kissed his neck. From deep inside him came a rumble: "Are you sure you don't want to…"

"No," I laughed. "Set me down."

He held me out and gently let my feet touch the ground. We dried, dressed, and then headed back to the camp. There were two tents set up and a fire. Vonn was tending the fire.

He turned, and an evil gleam lit up his eyes. In a teasing tone, he asked, "So, how was the lake?"

Immediately, heat filled my skin and I blurted, "We only swam."

Torric grumbled as he sat down, and Vonn hooted loudly. "I told you she wouldn't with me here, my friend."

My eyes flew to Torric. "You two were talking about it?"

Vonn laughed even harder. "What do they teach you girls in Renth? Sex is the most natural thing in the world. Especially between—"

"Vonn." Torric's harsh voice cut him off.

A sigh escaped me. The truth was, that I wasn't his wife. Maybe that didn't matter here in Glane, but back in Vella, my reputation would sink further. I smiled—I'd be more of an outcast than I already had been. Here, despite everyone knowing I was with Torric, despite being a healer with hair the color of fire, for that matter, I had respect. Even Vonn's teasing wasn't malicious.

After the meal, I crawled into one of the tents. When I realized that Torric wasn't coming in behind me, I leaned out to look for him. He was standing by a tree.

I climbed out and moved over to him, noting that Vonn was nowhere in sight. I frowned up at him. "What's going on?"

"I'm taking the first watch. Go to sleep. Once Vonn takes over, I'll come in. I promise."

I rose up onto the balls of my feet and kissed him softly. "Goodnight."

Before I could walk away, he hauled me against him and deepened the kiss. Fire ran through my veins and ignited my core. He growled, and his hand slipped around my hips and yanked me tighter against him sending a jolt through me as I realized the fullness of his desire. Without a thought, my legs wrapped around his waist. His tongue stroked along mine in a slow and sensual way. My heart sped up madly as need flooded my body.

Suddenly, there was a sneeze. I froze and drew away to look up at him with a blush, my legs sliding off his hips. In the heat of the moment, I had forgotten about Vonn.

Torric was grinning at me, his arm still around my hips as he ground slowly against me. My cheeks were in flames. I pushed at him and hissed, "Stop it."

Chuckling, he lowered me to the ground. I kissed his cheek one more time before I turned and slid inside the tent.

For a long time, my eyes just wouldn't close because I preferred his warmth instead of the cold quilt wrapped around me. I kept tossing and turning to try to find a position. When I thought that sleep would be impossible, I suddenly heard Torric singing softly. The sound of his voice comforted me like no other, and soon, I drifted away. I awoke later in the night to the feel of his arms around me as he tugged my body to his chest. Soon, however, surrounded by his woodsy, cinnamon scent, I was once again asleep.

Chapter Fourteen

The next four days were uneventful. We'd wake up early in the morning and start our day with a quick breakfast before cleaning the camp and heading out. Vonn and Torric would take turns keeping watch at night. Once Torric realized that my falling asleep easily was more likely when he was in our tent, he switched with Vonn so that he had the last watch. I didn't tell him how much I missed his warmth in the morning. However, Torric was more relaxed with Vonn around. I couldn't blame him; having someone to help him keep me safe made things easier for him. He slept better, and I was glad of that.

One evening I asked Vonn, "Have you always been in Fort Nyte?"

He smiled. "Zeer and I grew up in the village of Pheon. We'll be stopping there on our way to Kingshold. My assignment at Nyte was only temporary."

"Did you always want to be a spy?"

He broke into a friendly laugh and shook his head. "No. I'm not really a spy, Zianya, I'm more of a scout—but I do the occasional spying. During my assignment at the fort, my job has been to watch over the border. Every so often, the soldiers of Renth like to test their mettle against us. They cause some trouble, and there are a few spats, but eventually, when we don't try and push against the border, they back off."

"Why would they back off? Why not try to push the border closer to your side?"

Vonn's grin sent a shiver through me. "Because they push, but we stop them. They realize their casualties are not worth trying to expand into our territory."

I turned my eyes to Torric and I could see in his steady gaze that he was worried about how I would react to that. To be honest, I didn't know how to react to it. I hated fighting and death. But the soldiers of Renth were trying to break a treaty that had lasted for as long as anyone could remember, and as far as I was concerned, they were in the wrong. But their deaths... My feelings were very mixed when it came to them. Perhaps I was feeling like I no longer belonged in Renth. Or perhaps living outside those stifling walls opened my eyes a little.

I smiled, and Torric's emerald eyes became molten pools.

Vonn quipped, "No wonder you couldn't resist her. I couldn't if she gave me that sweet gaze."

Torric turned to him and frowned. "Stay away from her."

I was about to tell Torric that he shouldn't be so rude when Vonn chuckled. "You're so easy to rile, even knowing there's no reason to worry. This trip is going to be fun."

I rolled my eyes. "Not for me if you keep that up."

Vonn only laughed and tended the roasting wild chicken on the spit. I had tried to suggest my taking the cooking duties, but Vonn had insisted. And soon I realized why. His cooking skills over an open flame were amazing. So I let him take care of it, but I was finding being idle to be a bit disheartening. If the circumstances around my leaving Vella had not been so thrilling, I probably would have felt this sooner. But since being in Fort Nyte and having a chance to teach my herbalist skills, I found the monotony of the trek to Kingshold to be too much. There was no way that I could tell Torric and Vonn that.

My journey there was necessary. I knew it. Since being in Glane, I had grown to want to heal Donner. And I wanted to meet Sarine. She was Torric's sister, and I was hoping she'd like me. If she didn't, I wasn't sure what would happen with Torric and me. I probably would not have been concerned if what had happened back in Vella a few years ago to Ama didn't keep running through my mind. She was a sweet-tempered lovely girl that had been in love with Worren, a carpenter, and he with her. Worren's sister, however, had disliked Ama. It took some time, but eventually, Worren had tearfully broken it off with Ama and married a girl that his sister introduced him to at the bakery. Only the sister had been happy.

I took a deep breath and cleared my mind. Torric and Vonn were talking quietly about their watches for the evening. I was restless. There was nothing for me to do. Getting up, I walked away from the camp. Before I reached the edge, Torric was at my side. "Where are you going?"

I stopped and looked at him, confused. "You've never stopped me from going to relieve myself before. What's going on?"

"Nothing."

I arched an eyebrow. "Nothing? You're asking me where I'm wandering off to and you haven't before, so obviously, something is going on."

He scowled, and I folded my arms, waiting for his reply. Finally, he answered. "We're close to Deend. They tend to be a bit lawless."

I blinked in surprise. He stroked my cheek gently. "Not every place in Glane is as safe at Fort Nyte."

I leaned into him and smiled up at him. "I guess I was feeling so safe that I didn't think perhaps there were some places that were not."

"Come, I'll turn my back and guard you."

I blushed and glanced away. "Honestly, I was sneaking off for a walk. But if I have to go later, I'll tell you."

His eyebrows rose in surprise. "Why were you doing that?"

Pursing my lips, I looked away for a moment before I turned back and let out a soft huff of frustrated breath. "Because I'm sick of being useless. Sitting around while the two of you do everything is driving me crazy."

His rich laugh surprised me. His arms encircled me and his lips danced along mine as my body warmed against his. "Sorry. I should've realized that you'd hate not helping, lass. When we were alone, we'd at least share the cooking. Plus, you were on an adventure."

"Just give me something I can do," I moaned.

"How about when we stop, you and I go looking for wood together? I don't think Vonn will give up the cooking."

I grinned up at him and said, "Honestly, I don't want to take that over. I always end up overcooking one side when I cook over open flame."

Torric quickly pressed his lips to mine. His kiss was affectionate and tender. When he drew back, he touched his brow to mine and smiled down at me. I slipped a hand over his chest and let it rest over his heart, just to feel the steady rhythm. His hand slid up to cover mine, and for a long time, we stood there, reveling in each other's eyes.

When I came to my senses, I asked, "So tell me about Deend."

He frowned and drew me back to sit in the camp. Arranging me by his side, he held me with one arm.

Vonn looked over at us and gave a grin. The wild chicken he was cooking smelled delicious and my mouth watered just a little. My stomach gave a slight growl.

"Healers and their appetites…" Torric said teasingly.

I smirked up at Torric. "So does Donner eat a lot, too?"

My breath caught and I glanced at Vonn. I had no idea who knew that Donner was a healer, and saying that was probably a mistake.

Torric frowned. "Vonn knows, but you should be more careful."

I nodded.

He continued. "Now that I think about it, he does eat more than me."

"My mother and grandmother always ate a lot, too. I think it has something to do with how we heal."

"Don't worry," Vonn said. "We'll keep you well fed."

I grinned. "You might have to hunt more than you'd like."

Torric rolled his eyes. "As if I don't love to hunt."

Vonn took the chicken off the spit and cut it up, handing me both legs and a wing. Biting into one of the legs, I let out a little moan of delight. It was perfectly seasoned and juicy. Torric grinned at me before he dug into his own piece. When my eyes found Vonn, there was a proud gleam in his eyes.

After dinner, I got Vonn to let me help him with the cleanup. Torric decided to check the area to make sure there was no one around.

While alone, Vonn said, "I don't think anyone could ever thank you enough for coming to heal our king."

I grinned at him. "I didn't have a choice."

He laughed. "Ah, yes. Torric kidnapped you. You still had a choice, though."

As I organized his box of spices, I said, "No. Actually, once I see Donner, I won't have a choice. The need to heal can be overwhelming. Look what happened when you broke your arm."

His voice was rich and warm as he said, "Thank you for that, by the way."

I smiled. "It was my pleasure. I actually like healing. I suppose the only person I wouldn't want to heal is someone truly evil. Someone who preys on the weak."

He scrutinized me for several long moments before he asked, "So you would not heal them?"

I sighed. "Honestly, I'd hope that Torric would pull me away from someone like that. Not healing someone can be so difficult to do."

His eyebrows rose. "You're serious. It really is hard for you not to do it?"

I sat down and stared into the flames. "It is. I can do it, but it's at great, personal toll. If I choose to walk away, I can feel an ache inside for a long time."

He studied me a moment before he asked, "And if someone takes you away?"

"I'll hurt for a short while, but it isn't as severe. I can ignore it."

"Does Torric know?"

I let out a little huff of breath. "No. And I'd rather you not tell him. He seems to really care about my well-being, and I'd not want to upset him."

Vonn was quiet, and when I turned to look at him, I found him sitting there quietly, staring at me. Confusion filled me for a moment, but I smiled. "What?"

He hesitated, and when he spoke, it was in a very low tone. "I don't...want to get in the middle of this."

I turned back to the fire. "I wouldn't want you to. You're his friend. Some things I'll just have to learn for myself."

We sat quietly. I wondered how much longer Torric would be.

Suddenly, in a gentle voice, Vonn said, "I do know that he cares for you deeply."

A bright smile took my face and I turned him. "I know that much. I have no doubts about that. Vonn, don't worry about me."

He mussed my hair just a little bit, reminding me of an older brother. "All right, I'll try not to. But, I think that might be impossible."

"Why?"

"Because you're very sweet, and I might want to steal you away for myself."

I laughed and could feel my cheeks redden. When I met his eyes, he grinned at me, and I realized he was just teasing.

"Did I miss something?" Torric asked as he strode in to the camp. His emerald eyes darted from me to Vonn.

I grinned up at him. "Vonn was trying to tempt me to run away with him. Since you were taking so long, I was just about to say yes."

Vonn laughed as Torric frowned. He made his way over to me and sat close. His arm slipped possessively around me, and I peered up at him mischievously. I didn't know if Torric was in love with me as I was with him, but I knew I had a strong place in his heart and that he cared for me. It was enough. For the time being.

I awoke with a hand over my mouth and Torric's voice in my ear. "Shh. Don't say anything," he whispered fervently, "we need to be as quiet as we can while we move."

Nodding to him, I silently pulled on my riding clothes. I was happy to have taken up the habit of the women of Glane to wear pants. At least while I was traveling. When I slipped out of the tent, Torric and Vonn quickly brought it down and packed it away. I stood near Torric's horse, waiting for him. It took no time before he lifted me and set me in the saddle, and then he was on the horse behind me. Quietly, the horses picked their way down the trail. I wasn't sure what was going on, but the tension rolling off Torric made me very nervous.

I leaned back into him to take comfort in his warmth. His arm tightened around my waist. He leaned forward and softly whispered in my ear, "Don't worry, you'll be safe." I turned my face up to his. He looked down at me, part of his face in shadows, the rest lit up by the bright moonlight. His eyes were tender but full of determination. I reached up and softly stroked his cheek. His lips brushed against my temple. "I won't ever let anything happen to you."

"What's going on?" I asked softly.

He frowned, and I could see for a moment that he was debating telling me. I opened my mouth to ask him to stop coddling me, when he whispered, "When I joined Vonn for the watch, he decided to scout the area before he retired. About two hundred yards to the north of us, there was a group of bandits bedding down for the night. We decided it would be wiser to head out now and hope they don't find us. We'll stick to the trail for now, but once the sun rises, we're going to switch to another path through the forest. Don't worry. Get some sleep."

I leaned up and kissed his cheek. "And how am I to sleep knowing this?"

"There's no danger. If they'd seen us, they would've attacked us. Because of their size, they didn't think to scout out the area. Too arrogant. The only reason Vonn went so far was because of our proximity to Deend."

My eyes darted around. "Thankfully there's a bit of a forest here. If we were out in the open, they'd have seen us for sure."

He laid his cheek atop my head and whispered back, "Most of Glane is rolling hills of green and lakes broken by wooded areas. The Telleen runs through it, connecting all the lakes."

"I find it very beautiful," I said softly.

His hand caressed my waist. "I'm glad you like this land. It's your home now."

I chewed on my bottom lip. There was a question burning inside me. I wanted to ask it and to have an answer, but I was afraid of what he would think.

Taking a deep, shuddery breath, I said, "If I choose to return home to Vella, after I heal Donner, will you take me?"

I could feel him stiffen behind me. His hand on my waist, which had been softly stroking my belly, stilled. "Do you want to go home?"

Taking a deep breath, I very gently said, "I just want to know that I'm free to make that choice."

His arm around my waist drew me closer. He whispered, "I don't want to give you up, lass. But I will. If that's what you really want, I will."

I slipped my hand over his and squeezed softly. "I don't foresee me wanting to go home. I just wanted to know. Sometimes, I don't know my place here."

His voice was rough with emotion and his lips danced against my ear as he said, "Your place is with me. I'll always keep you safe."

I opened my mouth to tell him that I loved him, but then I closed it. The truth was, that I was afraid. I was afraid to tell him and find out that the depths of his emotions for me were not as deep. I was a coward, and so I clung to the balance he and I had formed.

He kissed my cheek again. "Go to sleep. We have a long road ahead."

"But you're awake. I don't want you to have to ride like this."

I could feel his hard body shaking behind me with a chuckle as he responded. "I've ridden far with you asleep in my arms. This time I have Vonn to keep me company while you snore."

My eyes went wide, and it took everything I had not to raise my voice. "I do not snore."

A laugh rumbled through him. "Yes, you do. Now sleep, my sweet lass."

For a while, I watched the moonlight dancing in the leaves. Little flashes of pale green fluttered in the dark as the cool wind twirled among them. It would not be much longer before those greens turned to vibrant reds, yellows, and oranges. I had always loved the fall on Mount Caden, and I wondered if I would miss having the mountains surrounding me. Once I healed Donner, I didn't know where I would go for the long term. I knew I would go back to Fort Nyte to train Kayla, but what about after that? Would Torric keep me with him? Or would I find myself some other home? I knew I could not go to the front lines in the war against Moritzan because there would be too many for me to heal. But I wanted to be useful here. And so, when the time came, I knew I would have to find something for myself in Glane.

Chapter Fifteen

Consciousness stirred me to life, and I was suddenly aware of cool air on my back and Torric's strong hands around my waist, gently pulling me off the horse and putting me on the ground. For a few long moments, he held my body against his solid form. His heat seeped into me as my soft curves molded to him. Pressing his lips to mine, he lay a slow and languid kiss across my mouth that burned the last of slumber out of me.

I blushed when Vonn cleared his throat. Pulling back, Torric grinned down at me.

"We won't have a fire. Vonn is going to take a nap, but first, we're going to eat some food from the packs."

"You should nap, too," I said.

His eyebrows shot up immediately. "I'm going to take the watch," he insisted quietly.

"I've been asleep, you haven't. I can look around and listen. If I hear anything at all, I'll wake you."

His eyes clouded with worry as he spoke. "If you miss something, you could get hurt before I wake."

I leaned to him and put my hand softly over his heart, and the fact that it sped up with that simple touch brought a smile to my lips. But he needed sleep, so I gently insisted, "I can do this."

"She can do this, Torric. Besides, it's only for a couple of hours." I twisted my neck to find Vonn watching the two of us with amusement twinkling in his eyes.

I beamed back at him and walked over to the saddlebags. Pulling out some cheese, fruits, and dried meats, I distributed them to Torric and Vonn. Silently, the three of us ate. We were close to the edge of the forest, and I could see the field through the trees. All that lay beyond were more of those vast and rolling green fields. I wondered how we were going to hide from bandits out there.

Once we finished eating, Torric and Vonn both got comfortable. I sat with my back to a tree and settled in to watch and listen. My life had become so different from when I was in Vella. I never thought that I would have to watch over a couple of warriors while they slept to make sure that bandits did not set upon us. I smiled to myself. Even though all of this was a little frightening, I was enjoying the adventure of it all.

As I sat there, every noise seemed like it could be an attacker. Several times, I almost woke them until I realized it was the sound of the wind in the trees or an animal in the bushes. Rising, I quietly walked around the area, checking out my surroundings. There was a small pond—if we didn't have to worry about possible bandits, I would have asked Torric to watch the area while I soaked in the appealing waters.

Turning to Torric, I studied him for a long moment. Usually, his sleeping face was so peaceful, but now it was tense, as if even in sleep he was ready to spring into action.

Eventually, I woke them and we set out once again. Soon we were riding at a canter across the hills. Once we had put some distance between the forest and ourselves, both men visibly relaxed. They were still a little tense, however, and I knew we weren't quite safe yet.

It was well past noon when we stopped to eat again. Once more, there was no fire, and we made a quick meal of the food we had on hand. Vonn kept his eyes behind us. Torric let his eyes roam the area on the other side of Vonn. I couldn't see anyone sneaking up on us, but I had to remind myself that anyone on the other side of any hill could hide.

I drew in a sharp breath as a ripple of panic ran through me. "Are bandits often a problem?"

"Yes," Vonn answered. "Certain areas of Glane have more than others. Near Fort Nyte, there are relatively few. However, in villages where most warriors have gone to help protect us from Moritzan, bands do spring up."

My mind whirled trying to find some solution. "Is there nothing to be done?"

"Keig's been talking about getting a small team together to hunt them." Vonn's voice didn't hold much hope in the idea.

I chewed thoughtfully on my apple. "But can a small group manage to root them out?"

The two warriors exchanged glances before Torric said, "It'll do some good. It won't stop the problem, though."

"But something must be done," I said, worry for the people of the land filling my heart. In Renth, there were a few bandit groups, but for the most part, it was safe. Well… safe as long as you didn't have red hair.

Vonn said, "You're right—something must be done, but as long as this war rages, very little can be."

"Is there no way to end it?"

"The war? We've tried negotiating for peace several times. Each time our ambassadors' heads came back to us. Moritzan wants our land—it's very fertile."

"And Renth?"

Softly, Torric said, "Do you think they'll stop with Glane?"

A tiny sigh escaped my lips, I shook my head, and suddenly my apple was not so appealing. I really didn't understand war. Then again, the need for violence also escaped me. If it wasn't for the fact that we had to keep going and I needed the energy, I may have just tossed the fruit to the side. Instead, I quickly finished before chucking the apple core aside.

Once we finished our lunch, we headed off again, keeping the horses at a steady pace. I knew we couldn't keep pushing the horses for too long, and so I suspected we were heading to a place that Torric and Vonn thought would be safe for the night.

I found Torric's found gaze on me. Arching up, I kissed him tenderly and his eyes softened into molten pools of emerald green that stirred the embers in my heart to fiery flames. Wishing we were alone, I rested back against him, my hand softly stroking his arm.

"Where are we headed?"

Torric's lips brushed my ear as he spoke, sending a thrill through me. "We're going to Gennon Lake. We'll replenish our water there, and we can swim."

"You and I alone?"

I found wickedness dancing in his eyes. "Almost."

Giggling, I shook my head. "*Almost* is not good enough for that."

He snorted. "I really need to free you from that modesty."

I snickered in turn. "You already have. However, this is as far as I'll be changing."

Pressing his lips to my temple, he embraced me warmly a moment. "Good enough. When we get to Kingshold, I'm taking you straight to my room."

I smiled and let my eyes wander the rolling green ahead. Snuggled into his warmth, it was hard to believe there was anything to fear. On that horse, it could have been just the two of us alone in the whole world. I closed my eyes a moment, and then I remembered the first time I awoke in his arms. I had been afraid at the time, but now I was grateful.

When we reached the lake, Torric and I immediately went for a swim. He made a point of running his hand over my body every chance he got. When we left the water, I was shivering, but not from the cool lake. As we dressed, our eyes met, and I melted at the desire I found in his gaze. I was sure it matched my own.

Our night was much like any other on the road—we ate together, with Vonn teasing the two of us from time to time. After I helped clean up, I slipped into the tent and curled up on my side. Normally I removed my clothing because I enjoyed the warmth of Torric's skin on mine, but after the bandits, I'd decided keeping my clothing on was wise. Torric curled up to my back, his fingers stretched across my waist, as he held me possessively to him.

I awoke to the sound of voices. As I peeked out of the tent, I found there were seven men standing on the edge of camp. Vonn and Torric had their swords out and were ready for a fight. My eyes went wide as one of the men spotted me and his leering face sent an icy spike of fear straight into my heart.

"We heard of two men travelling with a woman who may be a healer in disguise. There's a pretty price on her head. I'll take her for the reward."

Torric growled and pointed his blade at him. "You're the first to die." The venom in his voice caused a shudder to roll through me, and I wondered how the man could stand there and face my warrior with such a gleam in his eye.

His gaze lingered on me, and I glowered up at him. Suddenly, there was a glint of steel as Torric's blade slashed across the man's abdomen so deeply he fell to the ground with his entrails in his hands. The need to heal ran through me, but before it could even become a problem, Torric's sword drove into the man in a rapid stab that ended his life.

Chaos erupted. There were now six men remaining. Vonn faced three, as did Torric. Vonn moved swiftly among them. As three of them attacked at once, Vonn dodged the blade of one while deflecting the blade of another with a knife and cutting down a third with his sword. These men, whoever they were, had been counting on their numbers. However, Vonn and Torric were skilled warriors.

My eyes flashed to Torric, who was deflecting and parrying the attacks of two of the men he faced. The third was making his way over to me. He leered down at me and horror washed my soul gray as he brought up his sword. Then a blade punched out through his chest. The sword ripped out, and the man fell, dead, revealing Torric, who turned to loop back to the other two men.

Glancing at Vonn, I realized he now only had one opponent. The confidence our attackers once had seemed to falter. All that the three remaining men had left was the terror shining in their eyes. Torric struck down another. The final two turned and ran, and Vonn tore after them. I slipped out from the tent and went to Torric. He had a shallow gash across his chest. I reached for him, and he jerked back. "Not yet. We need to get this camp packed up and ready to go."

"But Vonn?"

Grimly, he said, "Vonn can take care of himself. I don't want to take any chances if these men have friends."

The two of us moved quickly, breaking down the tents and packing up our gear. Once we were finished and the packhorses were loaded up, Torric picked me up and placed me on the saddle. He stalked quietly around our perimeter, searching the night. When I saw him relax, I knew before I even laid eyes on him that Vonn was returning, looking no worse for wear. Torric swiftly swung up behind me while Vonn leaped into the saddle of his own horse. Soon we were off at a quick canter under the moonlight. The need to heal Torric was strong, but I fought it. Torric whispered in my ear, "You should sleep."

"I'm too anxious."

"There's nothing to be anxious about, lass. I will keep you safe. Vonn will, too."

I huffed in annoyance; he didn't get it. "I'm anxious for the two of you. I don't want anything to happen to either of you."

His lips pressed against my cheek. "I'll let you heal me if it means you'll sleep."

I grasped his arm tightly and let my healing energy seep into him as the ache that had been building in me released. It relaxed me to know that his wound was knitting back together.

When I discerned at last that he was whole, the darkness started to close in on me. It was strange how quickly I fell asleep since being with Torric. I decided it had to do with how safe I felt with him. As I fell deeper into the dark, there was the gentle flutter of his lips on my temple as I sunk into his warm embrace. When sleep finally shut down my mind, I didn't fight it the way I once did back in Vella.

Chapter Sixteen

When my eyes fluttered open, I could see a village in the distance. My best guess was that we would be there before midafternoon. Torric's hand softly caressed my belly as it grumbled, and he laughed in my ear. Before I could say anything, a small loaf of bread from the saddlebag appeared before me. I tore into it, feeling quite ravenous. "Is that Pheon?" I asked in between bites.

"It is."

"It's beautiful." And it was. Lying nestled among sloping hills of wheat, the walls around the village were a natural stone color. There was a river that edged around one side of the wall. The roofs were a splatter of various colors. Unlike Fort Nyte, there was no huge building. A thought struck me. "You don't have temples in Glane, do you?"

Torric laughed. "No, nothing like those monstrosities that you have in Renth. We do, however, have small groups that provide places of worship here."

"What do you worship?" It had suddenly occurred to me that they probably didn't worship the Great Spirit Caden as the people of Vella did.

"Each village has its own religion. Some of them, like Pheon, have many different religions within the walls."

"Well, that explains why there's no large temple. The people all go to different ones. But what do you worship?"

He paused for a long moment and we rode in silence. The gentle swaying of the horse's gait was hypnotic. When he finally spoke, I was startled. "I find religion to be confusing. There's so much suffering in the world, yet none of these Spirits do anything to alleviate it."

I contemplated what he was saying for a moment. "So you don't have faith. I suppose I can understand that. I used to go to Temple with the rest of my village every week. I sat and listened, but all Colm taught was hate. Honestly, I don't think the Spirits would condone his teaching. Then again, I'm not one of them. Still, I went every week."

His voice was soft, low. "Why did you go?"

My cheeks went red as I explained. "Because as long as I could go in there, it proved I wasn't an evil witch. I was terrified what the villagers would do to me if I didn't attend every week."

He scowled. "Like I said, I don't understand religion."

Sighing, I said, "I don't think it is all bad. I just haven't encountered religious truth yet."

He chortled. "Is there such a thing?"

"I certainly hope so," I fervently replied.

We rode on in silence. The land rolled by in soft hills of green, dotted with flowers that I ached to pick. The wind was cool as it swept the grass and flowers into a frenzy of swirling dances. I watched with a smile as Torric held me close to his chest. The dangers of the night seemed like a distant memory.

When we finally rode up to the gate, I let my eyes roam over its intricate carvings of warhorses and warriors engaged in battle. It was very beautiful—but unsettling. Vonn spoke to the guard and the gate opened to us. We made our way onto the winding roads through the village. Torric followed Vonn, and I had a feeling we were not staying at an inn. My suspicions were confirmed when we stopped in front of an elegant home.

A door opened, and a shapely woman, who was a few inches taller than me, strode out and met us with a friendly grin. She was closer to Vonn's age than mine, with warm brown skin, dancing black curls, and the most brilliant pale green eyes I'd ever seen. She was dressed in a simple gown of hunter green. Vonn swung off his horse, ran up to her, and kissed her deeply. I blushed and looked up at Torric, who grinned. "That's his wife, Meg."

Blinking a few times, I said, "I didn't know he was married."

"He is. I suppose we didn't think to mention it. They've been married for years. Come on." Now I realized what Vonn meant about Torric not having to worry about him with me. I watched the two with a smile as Torric swung off the horse and helped me down. Leading me up to the couple, we stopped just as Vonn pulled back to gaze down at his wife with loving eyes. Turning to us, he said, "Meg, you know Torric. This is his…woman, Zianya. She's come to help Donner."

The woman's eyes lit up as she looked me over. Suddenly, I found myself in her tender embrace. "Come on in, dear, you're very welcome. Let's get you fed. You're too skinny. What have you boys been doing to her? Riding her ragged? I'll get you a nice bath, too, dear, while the men take care of the horses."

She radiated warmth like the sun, so it was hard not to beam back at her. Immediately, I understood why Vonn loved her enough to make her his wife. With her arm around my waist like we were old friends, she led me into the house and up the side-stairs. Finally, she took me to a small bathing chamber. The tub would definitely not fit both Torric and me, but the brightly decorated room had flowers painted on the walls. The whole place was immaculately clean and smelled faintly of roses.

"Get yourself washed, dear, and I'll bring some clothing for you to wear."

Looking back at her, I said, "Torric knows where my things are."

Her eyes lit up with mischief. "Oh, I'm sure he does."

My eyes went wide and I could feel the flames in my cheeks. She laughed wickedly and left the room. When I noticed two faucets, I nearly danced. Renth must have been behind the times, because here in Pheon, they also had hot water. I turned it on and set about stripping off my clothing. It was easy to see they were going to need a good washing. But I decided to tend to that later. As I sunk into the water, there was a knock at the door, and Meg called out to me.

"Come in," I answered shyly.

She bustled in with some fresh clothing from my pack. Grabbing my old clothes, she paused to look at me. She strictly kept her eyes to my face, but I still flushed in embarrassment. Her gentle smile, however, set me at ease as she said, "I'll get these washed for you as well as some of the other clothing in your packs." She clucked her tongue. "Those men have no idea what a woman needs."

"You don't have to go through so much trouble."

"Nonsense. You have little dark circles under your eyes, dear. Let me at least do this."

With a chuckle, she slipped out of the room. Sinking deeper into the tub, I let out a long, slow breath. Spotting the soaps, I plunged under the water to wet my hair before I started scrubbing away with the lovely rose-scented products. Back in Vella, I had always been fastidious about bathing. However, since I had left, I'd had to forgo my daily bath for quick washings when I could. When I had gotten to Fort Nyte, I had reveled in having a bath again. I wasn't sure how long we'd stay in Pheon, but I was definitely going to take advantage of the bath here.

There was another knock at the door. Before I could speak, Torric opened the door and slipped inside. Fire flooded through me as I stared up at him "This bath is too small for your hulking frame to get in here with me."

The desire in his eyes as they traveled over my body seared me. "Then I guess I get to watch instead."

I laughed. "Oh, no you don't. Meg will be shocked!"

"I doubt that. She's off washing your clothes with Vonn right behind her. I've a feeling that there will be a delay in cleaning your clothing."

Heat of embarrassment washed over me. Torric laughed before he leaned down to kiss my temple. I let my eyes slowly slid over him before a smile fluttered across my lips. His hand traced along my cheek, down the column of my neck, before he slowly settled it on my chest. Softly, he cupped my breast before he started to knead gently, his eyes intent on my reaction. Desire filled my core, and I let out a little gasp as he squeezed my nipple. "Want me to wash you, lass?"

"Somehow, I get the feeling cleaning me is the last thing on your mind."

"Vonn and Meg are busy." His teasing voice didn't match the promise of heat in his eyes.

Giggling and shaking my head, I replied, "And I'm taking a bath in a very small tub. Not to mention, I don't want to get water all over her floor. So stop, please."

His thumb brushed over my nipple a few times before he tugged and a gasp tore from me. "Are you sure you're asking me to stop?" he rumbled.

"I'm sure. Now get out, you wild barbarian!"

His rich laugh filled the room as he walked out. When he left, I chewed on my bottom lip. Part of me wanted to call him right back in and let him give me a good and thorough washing. Yet, as I looked around, I had to once again realize that the tub was entirely too small, and I did not want to get water everywhere in the home of the woman who was showing me such sincere hospitality.

After my bath, I slipped out of the tub, set it to draining, and then dried myself off. Meg had grabbed my dark green skirt, cream-colored shirt, and my wide black belt. I dressed quickly, then braided my hair. It was still brown, but a bit lighter than when I had originally put the dye in. I had the feeling it would last until we reached Kingshold. As I examined myself in the mirror, I tilted my head. I had gotten thinner. Not a great deal, but enough that I noticed. I was never as thin as the girls back in Vella, but I wasn't overweight, either. I had to maintain a certain weight; the life that I used to heal was my own. In all the excitement, I hadn't eaten as much as I usually did. I'd have to rectify that before I met Donner.

I found Torric in the hall. He dragged me to him and kissed me soundly before heading into the bathing chamber to wash up himself.

Making my way down the stairs, I searched for Meg. I didn't look too closely, however, out of fear of finding her and Vonn being intimate. She came out of a small side room off the kitchen with Vonn grinning behind her. I blushed and glanced away, but I caught his kiss to her cheek before he left.

"Is there anything I can do to help?"

She smiled at me and pointed to the large table. "Sit here, I'll bring you some carrots to cut, and you can tell me all about yourself."

I found Meg easy to talk to, and soon I was regaling her with tales of my home and our journey as I sliced the carrots. She asked a few questions and glanced from time to time at my pendant. Finally, with the stew cooking, she put some tea and biscuits out for us. As I spread some jam over one of the biscuits, she asked, "Did Torric really give that to you?"

A flash of heat took my cheek. I really needed to get this under control. But dealing with friendly people was still new to me.

"Yes. It's just a token of affection. Everyone keeps making a big deal out of it, though."

She smiled knowingly. "I'm sure they are. Now, will you and Torric be sharing a room?"

I stopped midbite and looked at her with wide eyes. She laughed at my expression. I put down the biscuit and sipped some tea to fortify myself. "We will be." I said.

She grinned. "As you should. That man needs a woman, and I think you'll do nicely."

"Do you know where they've gone?"

"I sent the two of them to get me some supplies. They may as well make themselves useful while they're here. Otherwise, you'll spoil them. Don't pamper them, dear. A spoiled man is insufferable."

The expression she gave me was full of warning. Still, I laughed. "I won't. But to be honest, it's more like they spoil me."

"Really, now. Well, isn't that interesting?" I shrugged and she grinned at me before she added, "Eat some more. When I walked in, I could see your ribs."

I chuckled and took another bite to appease her. It was easy since it was so delicious—it practically melted in my mouth. The jam was an amazing mixture of sweet berries, and the butter perfectly balanced with salt. It would be so simple to stay here in the safety of Meg's warm home. I was certain it wouldn't take long for me to gain back the weight I had lost. But I also knew that we would have to head out eventually.

After dinner, which almost made me beg for thirds, Meg and I sat in the living room while Torric and Vonn went to check in with the village leader. Meg was working on a quilt, and I had to admire her color choices and patterns. I had little to do, so I pulled out the blank journal I had brought from Fort Nyte and began writing about my adventures. I started with the moment I had first seen Torric wounded. As I wrote about him, my cheeks went warm, and I realized just how much I had not viewed him as a patient, even when he was.

"You look flushed. Is anything wrong?"

I smiled at Meg. "No. Just dwelling on the past a bit."

Her perceptive gaze lit up with amusement and that was enough to drive me away. I rose and said graciously, "I think I'll head to bed."

She stood and surprised me with a heartfelt hug. I returned her embrace shyly before I dashed upstairs. The room I shared with Torric had a large canopy bed, a matching bureau, and a little writing desk. I stripped off my clothing and slipped into bed. I had forgotten to bring a chemise to sleep in. I somehow doubted Torric would mind such an oversight.

I awoke in the night to Torric's arms wrapping around me and hauling my back to his bare chest. I let out a soft sound of contentment and turned my face up to his kiss. As his tongue gently danced along the seam of my mouth, one of his hands slipped over my breast as the other trailed down past my stomach. I pulled my mouth away and let out a soft cry. "Torric, they'll hear."

He laughed and let his tongue run over the rim of my ear. "Can you hear them?"

"No."

"Then don't fear their hearing you. Once we leave here, I'll have to be good again. Unless you consent to our using the tent to—"

"No!"

He laughed as his fingers danced over me, and I gasped. With slow, insistent strokes, he brought fire to my body, and my back arched against his hard chest. One of his hands kneaded my breast, fingers plucking at my nipple, as his other hand slipped down my thigh, raised my leg, and then gently rested it atop his own. Gradually, his fingers trailed along my thigh and back to my core, drawing a cry of delight out of me. His attentions didn't stop. In fact, they became more demanding and intimate as his lips played along my neck. Soon I was crying out his name.

He drew me back against his chest and whispered in my ear, "I love when you call my name. Do it again."

And so I did. My cries rose, and I gasped for breath between each one. With a quick movement, he flipped me onto my back. In an instant, he was on top, and I slipped my legs around him as we joined in one powerful move of his hips. I gasped and looked up into his eyes. In the dim lamplight, his eyes gleamed brightly with fierce intensity. They bore into mine as I cried out again.

"That's it, lass, don't stop calling my name," he said roughly as he ground against me. I cried out in response, leaning up to capture his lips with a heated kiss. He responded by caressing my tongue with his in slow, sensual strokes, mimicking the movement of his hips. One of his hands slipped into my hair, and the other trailed down my side to my hip, hauling me closer, and pressing my legs open more. The fire of his movements brought me up to a fevered pitch. Tipping my head back, I screamed out his name louder than I ever had before. He grinned down at me with a wild gleam in his eyes and before too long, he roared out my name in response.

After a few long and deep breaths, he rolled onto his back, dragging me to rest on top of him. Gently pulling my face to his, he tenderly kissed my temple, my brow, my cheek, and finally, my lips. I stared down at him and he stroked back my hair. One of his hands slid softly down my back to rest on my bottom before he grabbed hold of me. Shyly, I admitted, "I missed this."

He grinned. "I know. So did I. We aren't far from Kingshold. There we'll share my room."

"How long are we to be in Kingshold?"

He softly wrapped a lock of my hair around his finger. "For as long as the king needs us. Or you ask to be sent home."

I smiled. "I won't be asking to return to Vella. I would, however, like to go back to Fort Nyte to finish training Kayla."

He stared at me for a long time. "You truly won't go?" he asked roughly.

"I won't. I promise. I know that I said before that I wanted the choice. I do still like knowing that if I ask, you'll take me. But I really know in my heart, I don't want to be parted from you, or to leave Glane."

He brought his lips to mine. The kiss was so warm and gentle, filled with promise and tenderness. I clung to him, and my heart swelled. His hands gripped my bottom and my thighs before he lifted me to sit astride him. At our joining, my back arched and I gasped his name. As he slowly brought me to release once more, I knew that I was safe with him. Forever.

Chapter Seventeen

The next day, Meg and I went out to the market. It was set up much like any other with its own cacophony of sounds and mixture of heady scents. There were various stalls along the walkway with vendors selling their wares. Torric had given me some money to buy anything I wanted for the trip or just for myself. I stopped by a vendor selling clothes and started to look over the shirts. Meg laughed and slipped her arm through mine. "Supplies first, dear."

With a soft exhale, I let her lead me off down the lane. We had about a five-day trip to Kingshold. We didn't need much, but we did need to resupply. Fortunately, I had Meg with me. She was a master at negotiating and knew all the best places to purchase goods. Once we were loaded down, she took me to a different stall that had the most amazing fabrics. I found a lovely dress in a soft, pale green that was more delicate than anything I had ever worn. For a moment, I pondered purchasing it. However, I usually wore skirts and shirts that were common among my class. Still, I eyed it from time to time.

She let out an exasperated sigh. "Oh, just buy it. Your man will enjoy it on you."

I turned shyly back at Meg. "Do you think?"

She grinned at me. "I know. Come on, buy it."

Looking it over one more time, I nodded and purchased it. We gathered our things and headed back to the house. As we walked through the market, the scent of spices—many I recognized, some I did not—turned the air into an intoxicating perfume. With all this to work with, it was no wonder that Vonn and Meg were such great cooks.

We were nearly back to their home when a girl came running up to us.

"What's wrong, Lizza?" Meg called out to her.

Lizza, an adorable girl with a riot of curly brown hair and huge brown eyes, turned up a tear-stained face to us. "It's Momma! She's having her baby too quickly, and she's in too much pain. The midwife sent me to get the medic."

Meg and I exchanged glances. I knew Torric wouldn't want me healing anyone because it could alert the wrong people to my presence. But I simply couldn't stand by and do nothing. Stepping forward, I gently placed my hand on the girl's shoulder. "Please take me to her. If she can be saved, then I can do it."

Meg's voice was uncertain. "Zianya, I don't think Torric would want—"

I shot Meg a quick glance. "He doesn't dictate whom I heal."

The girl exclaimed loudly, "You're a healer?"

"Hush now, Lizza. Take me to her."

We rushed through the winding streets. She brought me to a large gray house with a black roof. Opening the bright white door, I quickly followed her into the house. She headed for the stairs, and I picked up my pace as she led me into the third room. There, I found a young midwife holding an unresponsive baby and a dark-haired woman lying in bed, crying. "Please, my baby!"

Both of them needed my help. The consequences of healing two people at a time ran through me. It took a great toll, which is why I had told Torric I could only do one healing per day. But I couldn't sit back and do nothing, not when something like this was before me.

First, I rushed over to the midwife. The baby was my first priority; I could feel its little life fading fast.

"Please, give me the baby."

"Who are you?" asked the midwife. She was about twenty-five, with blonde hair and pale blue eyes.

"I'm a healer," I said, reaching for the baby.

She drew away from me.

"She's telling the truth, Carra," Meg said. "Give her the baby."

I took the little one in my arms and instantly let my healing energies sink into the still form. It was alive, but it was fading fast. Because it was so small, I knew I could still heal it despite how close to death the little one was. I infused the newborn with life, and I let out a small cry of joy when it started to squirm in my arms. I continued to work on the baby until it suddenly let out an angry squawk. I took a deep breath and handed the baby back to the midwife.

"Take care of him." With that, I moved on to the woman on the bed. I touched her. She was bleeding badly. She wasn't close to death…yet. I could tell if I didn't heal her, eventually, she'd bleed out and die. I let my healing sink into her. I could feel her wounds slowly knitting. My last thought before I drifted off was that Torric was going to be very angry with me.

The first thing I noticed was that my head was throbbing. The next thing I noticed were the hushed tones—and one of them was angry. But beneath the anger, I could sense worry. Fear. The other two voices were trying to calm him down.

"What if she doesn't wake up?" Torric's growl didn't mask the panic in his tone.

"Shh. My head is throbbing," I groaned softly.

Torric was immediately at my side, his hands gently running over my arm; I didn't need to see him to know it was his touch. My eyes fluttered at first, then opened, sending renewed shards of pain through my skull. I found Torric looking down at me, his eyes a war of fury and anguish. A weak smile took my lips. He tried to smile back, but he was so worried it came out wrong, twisted. He reached out to stroke my hair, but he must have remembered what I said about my head because he stopped.

"I thought I lost you." His rough voice bursting with untold emotions.

"I never said more than one healing was impossible." My voice was low but still brought pain to my pounding head.

"Zianya, you've been asleep for thirty-seven hours."

I closed my eyes to hide from the fear I saw in his gaze and moaned softly. "Sorry. I didn't mean to be out so long. But right now, I could use some tayden tea and food. Lots of food."

Meg said, "I can get that for you. Come on, Vonn. Let's leave them alone."

The bed dipped as Torric drew me into his arms. My head pulsated, but still, I curled into his chest. Softly, he stroked my hair. "Please don't touch my head, it really does hurt."

His hand slid down my back to rest on my bottom, holding me close to him. I felt safe and warm. Trying not to fall back to sleep, my eyes opened to find him staring down at me. The worry in his emerald eyes tore at my heart. He opened his mouth, but I cut him off. "I don't want to fight about it now. I hurt."

Pain flashed through that emerald I loved. "I wasn't going to say anything about this. We'll discuss it later. I was going to say I was worried about you. I am worried about you."

My lids fluttered closed as I sighed softly. "I'm sorry that I scared you."

"You didn't just scare me. You terrified me. You wouldn't wake up. I shook you and called your name, but you just slept."

I couldn't look at him when he sounded so full of fear. Of course, I really just wanted to keep still, and the light was bothering me. However, I couldn't tell him either of those things. If I did, it would only make it worse for him. So instead, I curled into his arms slowly, trying not to jostle my head, and tried to ease his fears. "This is why we don't normally heal more than one person in a day. I'll be fine. I just need lots of food and tea, like I said."

He growled. I would have laughed if it weren't for the pounding behind my eyes. While I wasn't sure that Torric's feelings were as deep as mine, I did know he cared about me deeply and that my safety was of the utmost importance to him. And I knew that he was prone to growling if he was upset. Or excited. From my position, I knew he wasn't excited. So I was sure the growl had to do with his fear of losing me.

"When you're well, we're having a long talk, lass."

I could hear Meg walk in, and I opened my eyes, smiling at her weakly as she poured me a cup of tea. Torric helped me to sit up, and I took the cup to drink the bitter brew. She had left some biscuits, butter, and jam for me to have while I waited for the meal she was making. I devoured them quickly before pouring a second cup of tayden tea. Torric's hand softly caressed my hip as I drank it. I felt as if he were trying to reassure himself that I was alive.

I could feel the pounding behind my eyes lessen just a little, and I let out a soft breath as the tension within me eased. I glanced over at Torric to find him staring at me. I smiled weakly. "I know. I'm sorry."

"No, you don't know!" he bellowed. When I winced from the pounding in my head, he closed his eyes and took a deep breath.

Mindful of my pain, he began again in a quiet voice, "You don't know. I thought you'd never wake again. I was going out of my mind."

"You know I always sleep after a healing. It stands to reason I would sleep longer."

"How should I know that? As far as I know from you, you shouldn't heal more than one person. What if you never woke up, Zianya?"

My eyes brimmed with tears at the anguish I heard in his voice. I didn't have an answer to that question. There was also no way I could explain to him how, if presented with such a choice again, I'd do the same thing. That poor mother and her sweet little infant—there was no way I could heal one and not the other. There was no way I could have walked away, either.

"This is why I can't be where the fighting is," I said softly.

"What do you mean?"

"I—" I broke off when Meg walked in with a tray full of meat and vegetables. My stomach growled loudly, and she grinned at me as she set the tray down and left quietly. Torric brought the food to me and I dug in with a furious need. After I devoured everything, I curled up on my side. I could feel the need to sleep taking me again. "I need to sleep a little more. Don't worry, I promise I'll be fine."

He tugged me to him. I felt myself drifting off. Softly, he stroked my back until I finally fell asleep.

When I woke some time later, it was dark. Torric was asleep beside me, his arm still around my waist. Gently, I lifted it and laid it by his side. Moving slowly, I slipped out of the bed and pulled on a robe. I made my way to the bathing chamber, and closed the door behind me. When I came back out, I found Meg standing in the hallway, her arms crossed, and a critical eye on me. "Do you know how much you scared us?"

I smiled weakly. "I didn't mean to. I just couldn't let one of them die."

Her hand softly grasped my arm. "I know. But you could have warned us that it would take so long."

"I didn't know how long I'd be out…or that I'd even be asleep that long. I've never healed more than one person. I know it isn't wise, that we shouldn't heal more than one person a day. I didn't know why."

She clucked her tongue. "Are you telling me you put your life on the line for strangers?"

"Well, I was pretty sure that I would live."

A frown twisted her lips. "Pretty sure? It would kill Torric if you didn't wake up. Didn't you think of that?" Her stern features reminded me of my mother when I'd been particularly naughty.

"I'll be honest—I didn't think of anything other than the fact that if I healed the mother, she'd never get over my letting her child die, and that if I healed the infant, both Lizza and her baby brother would be raised without a mother. I couldn't choose just one."

She sighed and shook her head, then came over and drew me into a warm hug. "You dear, sweet girl. Don't do that again! Do you understand?"

I looked away. It wasn't like me to be able to walk away from healing someone in need. I didn't think I could promise not to do it again.

Meg grabbed my face and turned it toward hers. "Do you understand?"

Frowning, I said, "I'll try."

She let out a frustrated sigh. "You need to think about the people who will be devastated if you die. Or the people who won't be healed because you made a choice that killed you."

"You mean like Donner?"

"Our king needs you, yes. But what of all the lives you could save besides his? Once you've healed him, you can set up a place where you can heal again. Also, you told me about Kayla. Who is going to teach her if you die? What about those of us who care for you, what will we do if you die from doing something foolish?"

I exhaled heavily and closed my eyes. She had many good points. Who knows how many lives would be lost if I died before my time? And my friends—they'd be sad. However...

"It's just so hard not to heal. And I felt like I could do it."

"I know. And you did do very good, dear. Please just be cautious in the future. Think of Torric and the rest of us before you make another rash decision."

I nodded and headed back to the room. I crawled slowly into the bed with Torric and burrowed into his side. His arm slipped around me and drew me close. I looked up to find him watching me. "Did you hear that?"

He smiled softly. "I did. She's right."

I cuddled into him. "I'm sorry. I didn't mean to frighten you."

"Listen, Donner might ask you to go to the front lines to heal our warriors. I'll talk to him and explain how you can't."

My lips contorted at the thought. "I can speak for myself, you know."

"I'm not saying you can't. But Donner can be persuasive, and you worry about people too much."

I laughed and nuzzled his neck.

He said, "Only when they took you to burn you as a witch had I been so scared."

"Well, I'm here now," I whispered in his ear, "and I'm not going anywhere. Well, except to see Donner."

"I feel like locking you up," he growled.

"If you want to drive me away, that's the way to do it."

He laughed softly. "Lass, do you think I'd actually follow through on that?"

A smile flirted with my lips. "No. I know you'd never hurt me. Of that, I'm absolutely certain."

He squeezed me to him "Just don't scare me like that again."

"I'll do my best."

He growled before falling silent. His arms drew me tighter to him. The tension rolling off him was palpable. I stroked over his chest, feeling his heart beating rapidly. Softly, I hummed to him as I ran my hand over his arm. It took some time, but eventually he relaxed under my gentle touch. We rested there, wrapped in each other's arms. I was no longer tired after all the sleep I had gotten, but soon he was snoring again. I watched the sky out the window. A few stars were twinkling in the night, and I could hear the wind playing with chimes in the distance.

I felt at peace, safe, and warm in Torric's arms. I wasn't sure how long he would want to be with me. For that matter, I wasn't sure if, for him, this was love or caring mixed with lust. And even though I loved him, I decided I didn't care how long I had with him. I wasn't going to dwell on tomorrow. Instead, I was going to enjoy what time I had with him. However long that time might be.

As the sky slowly brightened and the glorious colors of dawn painted the heavens, I felt Torric's arm slowly tighten around me. When I examined his face, he was asleep, but I could sense a stirring in him. Slowly, he woke. The more aware he became, the tighter his grip grew around me. Just as his eyes were about to open, I softly kissed him. His kiss was slow and languid. And then, it was urgent.

Desire flooded through me. He rolled me onto my back and deepened the kiss. My hand slipped through his hair and down his back, fingertips caressing every defined muscle. He was still in his pants, having crawled into bed dressed after I woke. My hands slipped around to the front of his leathers and started on the laces. Suddenly, he grasped my hands and pulled away from the kiss. He frowned down at me. "Lass, you're not ready for this."

"You don't know that." I pouted up at him and he let out a soft laugh. Gently, he stroked my hair back and kissed my brow. Then he wrapped me up in a blanket.

"Your head is still aching."

I frowned up at him. "How would you know that?"

He put his finger right between my eyebrows and softly massaged the area. "You get the cutest little furrow right here when your head is aching."

I blinked in surprise. "That's quite an observation."

A bright twinkle of amusement sparkled in his emerald eyes. "I miss very little when it comes to you. I'll go get some breakfast and tea from Meg, and I'll be back. Wait here." He kissed my temple gently and got up. He paused at the door and glanced at me. A flash of delight tore through me. He shook his head. "You make it very difficult to let you be."

"Good. Because I don't want you to ever let me be."

His smile warmed my heart. For a moment, it seemed like there was something he wanted to say, but then he shook his head and walked out of the room.

Looking around the area, I had a feeling that I would not go out for a couple of days, at the very least. Lying back down, I took a deep breath and decided it was for the best. Despite my advances, I felt worn down, and my head pulsated with each beat of my heart. I wouldn't tell them, but a few days of rest were just what I needed.

Chapter Eighteen

After two days trapped in the room with only the bathing chamber as my one escape, I was going crazy. Torric was worried, and since my headache was lingering, I didn't fight him on it. It was on the third day that Torric and Vonn went out. After I washed, I quickly dressed and went downstairs, where Meg was kneading dough in the kitchen. She smiled brightly when she saw me. "There you are. I was wondering if you'd ever leave that room again."

I grinned and replied sweetly, "Don't blame me. Blame Torric."

She frowned. "You know very well it was your own fault."

With a shrug, I grabbed some bread before taking a seat at the table. Watching her as she took the dough, put it in a bowl, and covered it with a small, colorful tea towel to let it rise for a bit, I smiled. Meg made me wonder what it would have been like to have an older sister. She was warm and kind, and in these days that I had been in Pheon, she had made me feel most welcome. I frowned.

"What are you thinking of, dear?"

"That I'm going to miss you." My breath snagged on the last word, and I turned away to hide the moisture in my eyes.

She stopped and smiled warmly at me. "I'll miss you, too. So you have to come and visit."

Taking a deep breath, I nodded. "I will. I promise."

Sunlight streamed through the window, and I peeked out. The sky was bright, and the air that came through the opening was clear and clean. It was a perfect day, and I was tired of being in the house. My eyes drifted back over to Meg, but she was busy working. I debated. On one hand, I wanted to help her. On the other, I was so tired of the enforced rest that I needed to get out before I lost my mind. "Meg, do you need anything at the market?"

She paused and looked at me. Then she laughed with a twinkle in her eyes. "You're tired of being in here, hmm? If I let you go out and buy what I need, do you promise not to run off and heal someone?"

A scowl took me. "You know I can't promise that. If someone is before me in need of healing, I can't help it."

She narrowed her gaze. "All right, if someone is wounded right before you, I understand. However, if you hear of someone injured, will you please at least come get me first?"

Delight flushed through me and rang in my voice. "That I can do."

She regarded me for a long moment and then added, "Torric's going to be angry, so hurry back before noon to soothe him."

I bounced up and hugged her tightly. "Thank you."

As I turned, she called out, "Wait! Let me tell you what I need and give you some money."

After I wrote down her list and had some money in my pocket, I set out with a spring in my step and a satchel on my hip. It had been some time since I had gone shopping alone. Back in Vella, before Torric had taken me, I did everything alone. And while I did not miss that lonely life, I was excited to go wandering off in a village alone. Pheon seemed like the perfect place to roam.

As I made my way down the lane, I moved along unhurriedly as I took everything in. When I had gone with Meg, I hadn't had the opportunity to really pause and examine the buildings. Whereas Vella had very plain buildings with bright red doors, Pheon was alive with color. I saw homes in all manner of colors. Blues, reds, greens, yellows, and every other color in between lined the road. Many of the homes had intricately carved doors. Some had brightly painted columns that held aloft large second-floor verandas covered in plants. I wanted to climb onto one of them to see if they were gardens.

The market was much as I remembered. I found the fabric store and perused the various bolts of some of the most amazing weaving I had ever seen. I let my hand softly caress the fabric and wondered at its softness. I smiled and imagined a dress made out of the vibrant blue. I was quite sure Torric would like it on me.

"Are you looking to make a dress?" A sweet-faced, elderly woman came over to me. She was just a little shorter than I was and had amazingly bright amber eyes. She smiled, and it was so infectious, I grinned back.

"Sadly, no. I'm just browsing."

Her eyes lit up in recognition and she beamed. "You're that healer."

"What?"

With knowing eyes she said, "I saw you with Meg the other day, and I heard from Lizza how you saved her mother. I'll give you the fabric, dear. That you'd do such a thing for Cyn and her family is a rare thing. From your hair, I suppose you're trying to hide you're a healer and yet you exposed yourself."

"Healing is a gift that always needs to be freely shared," I repeated my mother's words.

"Indeed. Are you shopping today?"

I beamed brightly at her. "Just picking up some things for Meg. But your fabrics were so lovely I had to look."

"You go and shop. When you come back here, I'll have some fabric ready for you to pick up."

I felt tears spring to my eyes. In Vella, no one ever praised me for a healing other than my family. Here, in this faraway place, a woman was so grateful for my work, she wanted to give me a gift. I wiped my eyes and took her hand. "You don't have to do that. But I do thank you."

"No, you're right. I don't have to do this. I want to. Now, get out of my store so I can get to work."

I laughed and gave her a grateful hug, which she warmly returned. After I got her name, I said, "Thank you, Cera, for your kindness. I truly appreciate it."

She smiled back at me and I turned, strolling out into the hustle of the market. I made my way along the well-worn path and stopped next at a spice trader's store. Within the shop, the air was heavy with the rich scent of the exotic spices. I told the man behind the counter what Meg had wanted to purchase, and I wandered while he prepared them for me. While there were many seasonings I knew, there were also many exotic spices and blends that I had never encountered before. Heady scents filled the air, and their many colors were rich and vibrant. By the time I had my purchases in the satchel and paid for them, I loathed leaving. There were other items on my list, however, and so I was off.

I spent the better part of my time slowly wandering from shop to shop. However, as I moved along the way, a cold shiver ran up my spine. Glancing around, I searched the crowd but didn't notice anyone. Deciding I was being a bit paranoid, I shook it off and moved on to the next vendor to order some flour for delivery to Meg's home. I smiled as I let the chattering of vendors and consumers flood over me. It seemed that, just like the market back home, people exchanged all sorts of news and gossip as they shopped.

"Healer!" A small girl's voice rang out behind me, and I turned to find little Lizza running up to me. Her eyes were bright with her happy smile. I paused and waited for her.

"Lizza, you look happy. How're your mother and baby brother?"

Her happy smile turned into a huge grin as she replied. "Very well, thanks to you!"

Her smile was so sunny that I found myself grinning down at her. Gently, I stroked the top of her hair. Tilting my head, I asked, "Would you like to go get a sweet?"

Her eyes lit up. "Yes, please!"

She skipped beside me as we walked down toward the baker who had set up a little stall to sell some confections. Once we arrived, I waited while she picked one. I chose a little chocolate cake with creamy vanilla frosting. Armed with our goodies, the two of us found a bench and ate. The cake was so delicious that I craved another piece before I even finished the one I was eating. Lizza ate hers up in three quick bites. She chattered to me about how adorable her baby brother was, but also how he cried about everything.

I chuckled. "Well, that's how they tell you they need something. Make sure you take good care of the two of them."

She jumped off the bench grinning and said in a singsong voice, "I will."

As she ran off, amusement threatened to bubble out of me. I wondered briefly if I would have a child one day—and if I did, what he or she would be like. Would that precious one be a healer like me? I didn't know. I did know that I hoped that I was still with Torric when that day came.

Rising, I stretched before heading off down the market way. Inhaling the rich and varied scents while listening to the town gossip, I was content. Back home, I had never been content. Going to the market was usually a hurried experience where I got what I needed and got home as quickly as possible. Here, I was enjoying the warmth of this village.

An arm suddenly wrapped around me and I looked up to find a strange man staring down at me with a grin that sent a shiver down my spine. He had long, matted, oily black hair held back in a braid. A long, scruffy beard covered most of his face, and his gray eyes had a wild gleam to them. He chuckled down at me, his putrid breath turning my stomach, and then he started hauling me along. In a quick, low voice he whispered, "Don't scream now. I really don't want to hurt you. But I will. I will."

As fear sunk its ugly claws into me, my mouth was too dry to even swallow. My eyes darted around wildly. As we passed the fabric shop, Cera started to call out to me and then frowned. I met her eyes and beseeched the Spirits to make sure that my fear got through to her. And that she conveyed to Torric that I'd been taken. Again. I was such a fool. I thought that here, in this village, I'd be safe. Instead, a strange man was roughly dragging me into an alley. My bones rattled as I shook. He laughed in my ear.

I took a deep shuddery breath. "What do you want?"

"Why, I want you, healer." His voice was low, but it rang with all the hallmarks of an unsteady mind. That was one thing I couldn't cure.

"What do you want me for? Does someone need healing?" Instead of replying, he cackled as we made our way down one alley and into the next. My breath started to come in quick gasps. Even if Cera had seen which alley we went down, who knew where this man would drag me? Once he brought me into a building, Torric would not be able to find me—at least not in time.

I tried to stall. "So someone does need healing?"

He grinned down at me, and his sour breath washed over me. I gagged as he answered, "Many people need healin', and you're gonna make me a fortune!"

My eyes went wide in surprise. "You…what're you going to do with me?"

"Once we get to my cart, I'm tyin' you up and we're headin' out of here. We'll travel together, you and me. When there are people needin' healin', you'll do it. And I'll reap the rewards." He gave me an appreciative grin. "I'll wait, but eventually you'll learn to want me."

My stomach turned, and I almost retched right there. I started to struggle. He cursed and tugged me on. I dug my feet into the ground, but he just dragged me. When I opened my mouth to scream, he clamped his hand down over my lips and held me firmly. In my ear, he whispered, "If you don't stop bein' a hassle, I'll find excitin' ways to hurt you."

I quaked, ceased my struggling, and let my body become deadweight. He crouched down and slung me over his shoulder. Fighting against the tears that threatened to consume me, I tried to figure out what I could do. Once I was in that cart, chances were I was never getting away. Taking a deep breath, I quickly twisted my body and shoved my hands against his head. He dropped me, and I scrambled to my feet to run. Grabbing my arm, he slammed me against the wall. My head cracked, and pain shot through me. I glared up at him defiantly and he backhanded me across the cheek. My head turned violently with the force.

"If you don't unhand my woman, I'll kill you slowly and painfully," a growling voice threatened. A voice that sent a thrill of recognition through me. I turned to find Torric standing there. His emerald eyes were on my would-be abductor, promising violence.

My attacker's eyes went wide and the scent of urine filled the air. He turned tail and ran. Torric tore after him in a flash. Grabbing the man by the back of the neck, he whipped him to the left toward the building and slammed him into it.

"You hit my woman." Torric's voice was low and deadly.

"I-I didn't know she was your woman! I'm sorry!" The man cowered against the wall and sunk to the ground.

Torric raised his fist, and I hurled myself at him. Putting both hands on his chest, I said gently, "Stop. Stop! He's just a deranged man who thought he'd make a profit."

His glowering eyes were on the trembling wretch, but slowly they moved to me and softened. His voice almost broke me. "He hit you."

My heart thumping wildly, I smiled up at him. "That's what crazy people do. Let him go and take me back to the house. I'm tired, I'm hungry, and I just want to feel safe."

His glare turning back to the man, Torric gave a jerk of his head. Behind me, I could hear the pounding of his running feet moving away from me. My warrior watched him with a savage gaze for so long, I thought he'd go after him before he turned his gaze down to me. The change in his furious expression was immediate. Such warmth pooled in his eyes that relief flooded through my heart in a wave. Slipping his arm around me, we started back toward the house.

A tremble ran through me as I asked, "How did you find me?"

"Meg had told me you were shopping. I was on my way to find you when an older woman ran up to me. She said she'd seen me with you and asked if I would help you. Then she told me how that man dragged you off and pointed out the way. I'm sorry I was late."

I smiled up at him. "You were just on time."

He stopped and looked down at me. From the searching of his eyes, I knew he was taking in the freshly forming bruise on my cheek. Reaching up, I gently stroked his face and warmth flooded my heart. I loved this man so much that my heart felt like it would burst out of my chest. But I held onto it. I was too afraid to tell him. Lightly, he kissed my temple on the opposite side of the bruise. With a frustrated sigh, he slipped his arm around me again and we headed back toward the market. "What are you thinking?"

His eyes held tender affection, laced with gentle amusement as he said to me, "That you know how to get your pretty little ass into trouble."

I started to giggle as we left the alley and finally entered the market. Cera was waiting by the entrance. I left Torric's arms to embrace the woman gently. She softly fluffed my hair a moment before drawing back and looking at me. "My dear, can you not heal yourself?"

"Sadly, that's one thing I can't do. I do have a salve that I'll put on it that'll help it heal a bit faster than normal. Thank you, Cera. If you hadn't sent Torric my way, there's no telling what…" I broke off, unable to continue the thought.

"There, there, child. Everything is fine now. Plus, I have your fabric all wrapped up for you."

"What fabric?" Torric asked.

"Something pretty for a pretty girl. My gift to her for healing Cyn." With that, she handed me a large bundle that Torric intercepted and carried for me. When we reached the house, Meg rushed out to me and pulled me into her arms. Vonn stepped down off the steps and looked me over. The worry coming from both of them thickened the air.

"How did you know?" Torric asked as Meg ushered me into the home.

Vonn replied, "Lizza came by. I was just on my way to join in the search for her when Meg spotted you from the window. Is she all right?"

I laughed. "*She* is fine. Just a little bruised."

He frowned at me. "We can't let you out of our sight."

With a grin, I let them guide me into the house, where I was sure the three of them would fuss over me.

Chapter Nineteen

Two days later, with the bruise still bright on my face, we left the village and the warmth of Meg's hearth. Despite the attack by one disturbed man, I really enjoyed Pheon, and I would miss its spice shop. Leaning back, I inhaled Torric's scent, which I had come to crave. His arm tightened around me and drew me close to him again. I smiled and let his enticing heat seep into me. Riding in his arms was second nature now. The safety of his warmth surrounded me like a comforting blanket.

The rolling hills were a never-ending canvas of colors, and for the next four days, we rode harder than before. We'd eat the food in the saddlebags for lunch. Torric and Vonn would ride until there was barely enough light to set up a camp. I had a feeling they were making up for time lost because of the healing I'd done that had me down for a few days, not to mention the run-in with the irrational man. Torric hadn't taken his eyes off me since then, and the last night we had made love before setting off, there was a powerful intensity to him, as if he were branding me as his. A small part of me wondered if he was worried about losing me. There was no way I could explain to him that the only way he was getting rid of me was if he broke this off. Whatever this was.

I cursed my inexperience in relationships with men. Despite being a keen observer of people, when it came to Torric and me, I was at a complete loss. I wanted to broach the subject of my love for him, but each time, ice would shoot through my heart, staying my words with fear. Instead, I clung to my feelings and reveled in the warmth between us for as long as it would last. Because of this, I both longed and feared our arrival at Kingshold.

On the fifth day, by midmorning, I noticed that each time we went down a hill, there was less of a slope than when we had gone up it. Each hill rose higher and higher. Finally, we reached the crest of an especially high hill and paused. The valley was deep. There was a large river rushing down through the green swell of hills. It wound its way through the large valley and straight into the largest city I had ever seen.

Kingshold was nothing like I could have imagined. The large, shiny, black walls loomed around the sprawling city. Buildings of various sizes sprouted up everywhere—and the colors were amazing. Rich reds, greens, blues, yellows, and every other color I could conceive. In the center was a large, black castle. The design was not one I had ever seen or heard of before, an octagon. Each corner of the castle had a guard tower—which could hardly be considered "towers" compared to the massive tower at the castle's center. It rose so high, I swore it could touch the clouds.

"Kingshold," Torric said softly in my ear. "Before the war, there was no wall around the city. But when things got bad, we had to build it."

"It's magnificent."

Torric nipped my ear before asking, "You ready?"

"As ready as I can be."

With that, we picked our way down the hill and into the valley. By late afternoon, we finally stopped in front of the huge gate. I marveled at its scrollwork, a carving of a large dragon, staring down with twin emerald eyes. Those eyes caused a shiver to roll through me. A sudden awe stilled my soul as I realized those stones were actual emeralds and not painted rocks. Vonn went to speak with the guard at the gate while I stared up at it in a reverent silence.

"Impressed?"

I laughed. "Intimidated."

Behind me, his chuckle shook his body. "Well, it is supposed to be daunting, lass."

When the gate opened, I was thankful that the dragon disappeared from view. We made our way into the city. It was loud with the voices of its people. The air was heavy with the scent of the river, spices, and cooking fish.

As I looked around, I noticed many people gawking at me. My hair was a light auburn now; not much longer and it would be flame-red again. I wondered if they knew what I was. I smiled and stared ahead as I tried to ignore their gaping. The streets were packed, and the horses moved at a slow pace. My eyes sought out the castle, and I wondered if, when I met Donner, I'd still be happy to heal him. Despite the kindness of my new friends, a part of me was leery of people. What if all of it was a lie?

No. As I turned my gaze back to Torric, I knew one thing wasn't a lie. Without a doubt, Torric cared for me deeply. He would never let something bad happen to me, and as long as I was with him, I was safe. I also felt sure that Torric had not lied to me. Glane was not full of evil, as the gossip of old ladies had led me to believe. Rather, it was full of all types of people, just as Renth was. I had to trust what Torric had told me of Donner.

We finally made it to the castle gates. The scrollwork on this one was a large jungle cat with fierce sapphire eyes — real sapphires, I might add — scanning all those who dared to enter. For some reason, this creature did not make me tremble. In fact, there was something noble in its expression.

These guards knew Torric and Vonn on sight, and the huge gate immediately opened to admit us into a large courtyard. Within the courtyard was a ring of white birch trees. Grass grew in geometric shapes cut into sections by white stone walkways.

"Torric!"

I looked up to see a young woman in red come running down the stairs that clung to one of the walls of the castle. Her hair was long and blonde, and her clingy dress accentuated her svelte body. I was surprised to feel a stab of jealousy. I had never been the jealous type, but this girl inspired it within me. She barely gave me a glance as she beamed up at Torric.

"Well, aren't you going to kiss me?" she asked eagerly.

I nearly growled in anger. Torric tightened his grip on me and looked down at the girl. His voice held a note of irritation. "Gemma, I've never kissed you before, I'm not going to start now."

She frowned up at him. "You're no fun at all." Then, she turned to me. Her blue eyes ran up and down my form, clouded by complete disdain. "Who's this?"

With pride, Torric said, "This is Zianya, the Healer of Vella. She's come to save Donner. So mind your manners."

The annoyance in the girl's eyes told me she did not intend to do any such thing, but she said sweetly, "Yes."

Torric swung down from the horse and then reached up to pull me down. He set an arm around my waist, which elicited a hateful glare from Gemma. I decided to ignore it. I grew up with people hating me—what was one more?

As an attendant took care of the horses, Vonn excused himself. I had a feeling he was going off to make a report about Fort Nyte. The three of us took the stairs Gemma had come down and entered into the castle. I gasped at all the green marble covering every square inch of the room. "Is every room like this?"

Sashaying toward the middle of the room, Gemma turned her eyes to me. "Of course not. This is just the secondary entry. The marble here isn't as fine as the other areas of our home."

I gritted my teeth and said sweetly, "Thank you."

On the other hand, Torric didn't seem happy with her tone. "Gemma…" he said warningly.

"What? It isn't my fault she's not refined enough to understand such things."

I barked out a laugh. Torric turned his eyes to me before he started to laugh as well. He pulled me tightly to him and kissed my brow. I spied Gemma's caustic gaze heating up with hostility. With her desired effect ruined, she sneered at me. I smiled brightly at her and leaned up to kiss Torric's cheek lovingly. "I'm tired," I said with a yawn.

"I'll show you to your room. It's close to the servants but very nice. Where the healers used to be stationed." Her tone led me to believe she thought a healer was no better in her eyes. I pitied any servants that attended to her.

I was about to answer when Torric said gruffly, "She shares my room, and we're heading there now."

The shock in her eyes as she gaped at Torric quickly turned to fiery fury when she glowered at me. Once, I would have tried to be sweet. Maybe tried to hide my feelings. When I was in Vella, I had become so used to hiding my thoughts, my emotions. During this trip, I was becoming bolder every day. So instead of trying to ingratiate myself to her, I grinned at her and curled closer to Torric. Not because I wanted her to be jealous, but rather I was staking my claim. Maybe it wasn't kind, but I felt in my soul that if she had the opportunity, she'd try to take Torric from me.

With Torric drawing me along, we made our way down the hall. Eventually, the green marble gave way to white. As I studied my surroundings, I realized that this place was very old. It was easy to see that at one time, this place probably sparkled and shined, but now it was dull. The tables and the pieces of art I found along the way were in need of a good dusting. I had a feeling there really were not that many servants anymore. "This was built a long time ago?"

Torric grinned down at me "Before the war. From what I know, there used to be a thousand servants here. Now there are barely fifty. Our people went from being farmers and nobles to warriors in order to protect their lands. The many lords and ladies that once roamed these halls are, for the most part, back in their homes, protecting their people with what few spare warriors there are to watch over villages. There are still a few on hand at the court, but they rotate out."

I didn't know what to do. I could help Donner, but I couldn't save a kingdom. I couldn't go to their front lines because I was one healer. My heart grew heavy. All I wanted was to find some way that I could do something to end this war, but my mind was blank.

Suddenly, Torric pulled us to a stop and he turned me to him. He raised my chin and looked down at me. He kissed my brow before he said, "Stop what you're doing."

I arched an eyebrow, "Just what am I doing?"

"Trying to find a way to heal a kingdom," he said gently. "You're one woman. You heal our king, and that will help us. Stay here in Glane, and that will help us. We'll go to Fort Nyte and you can finish teaching Kayla. That will help. Please, my little healer, stop."

Searching his eyes, I knew he was right. There would always be a part of me that would want to help, but there was only so much that I could do. As that beautiful emerald gaze roamed my face, he must have seen something because he nodded and guided me to a set of stairs. The first set of stairs was fine. I was not thrilled with the second. By the fourth, I was ready to drop.

He must have noticed because he suddenly swept me into his arms as he climbed the last flight. "What is it with stairs?" I grumbled. "I can climb a mountainside, but I'm wheezing from all these stairs. Of course, when I climb the mountainside, I tend to pause and gather plants."

He laughed. "That's probably the reason. A few months in here and you'll be fine."

I grinned. "Or I'll be pausing every three flights." He started down the hall and I said, "I can walk from here."

He gently bit my ear and I let out a little cry. "No, I'm having a lot of fun carrying you."

With a quick pace, he continued down the hall, passing a few doors that were widely set apart. Finally, he stopped at a door and opened it up. As I tried to glance inside, he turned so that I was facing the hall. We slipped inside and he set me down. I moved in and poked around his quarters. They were large. The immediate area I was in was an enormous room with a seating section to the left of the door. To the right was a large table with four chairs. The room was utilitarian, however, with a weapons workbench at the back wall. The furniture was masculine and perfunctory. The floors, walls, and ceilings were all a rich dark-stained wood, and lacked personal touches or embellishments. While well-made furnishings filled the room, I felt it needed something.

"What do you think?" he asked hesitantly, which wasn't like him. When I glanced up at him, I could tell he was anxious for what I really thought.

"I think it's very masculine," I said tactfully.

"Then feel free to add what you'd like."

My eyes went wide. "Isn't that…invasive?"

He pulled me close and whispered, "I want you to be comfortable here. Happy."

I could feel my cheeks flush. "I am happy."

Wickedness gleamed in his eyes. "Want to see the bedroom?"

Stifling a giggle, I said, "I have a feeling you have an ulterior motive."

He ran his teeth over my neck, eliciting a shudder that ran through me. "I might."

"I'd like a bath first, though."

He licked his lips a moment before he said, "Then let me show you the bathing chamber, my little healer."

After a bath—and after we splashed water all over in a frantic need to make love—I slept for a long time. When I woke, I was starving. Dressing in a green gown that Torric must have left draped over the back of a chair, I left his bedroom, which was as practical as the rest of the chambers. When I opened the door, my mouth began to water from the luscious smells of exotic foods. My stomach growled loudly, and Torric laughed from a chair close to the bedroom door. There he was watching me with his emerald gaze churning with emotions I couldn't even begin to fathom. "What are you doing?"

He rose, crossed over to me, and took my hand. "I was waiting for you. Come on. Let's eat, and then I'll take you to meet my sister."

Fear gripped me. "Today?"

His mouth twisted in a wry smile. "Well, when else?"

I fidgeted anxiously. "I don't know why I'm so nervous. Am I to meet Donner today, too?"

He nodded and guided me to the table. We feasted on some of the finest food I'd ever known. We didn't talk, but there was ease and warmth flowing between us. Sometimes I'd raise my eyes from my food and find him studying me. When my cheeks would redden, he'd let out a chuckle. The simple times with Torric always filled my heart with joy. Our journey on the road had been full of so many adventures that it was nice to just be quiet and close.

After we finished, he led me down the hall. I was grateful to be with him because I was beginning to think that the castle was a labyrinth. Eventually, he led me to a large, ornately carved door. It was adorned with intricate flowers and leaves. Then it dawned on me: this was the queen's chambers and probably had been since the castle was originally constructed.

Torric knocked softly, and I nervously gripped his arm. My stomach dropped as the door opened and a tall woman stood there with a warm smile and emerald eyes. Even if she didn't have the same midnight-black hair, I would have known her to be Torric's sister. Her features were much like his, only soft, feminine. Her belly was round with child—she probably only had a month or so left. When her eyes fell upon me, she smiled but quickly turned her gaze back to her brother.

"What? No kiss for your older sister?" she asked in a rich voice, which was a lighter, feminine version of Torric's.

Grinning, he kissed her on the cheek and then hugged her tightly. Softly, he set his hand on her belly and looked up at her. "And how is the little one doing?"

"Oof. Kicking me nonstop, giving me indigestion, and telling me that he or she is almost ready. Now, who are you?" Her green eyes turned to me as she smiled. Either no one had told her of my arrival, or because of my slightly darker hair color, she didn't realize.

Torric slipped his arm around me, and this caused Sarine's eyes to go wide. Her emerald gaze darted between the two of us for a moment before settling on me. I smiled nervously as Torric said, "This is Zianya, the Healer of Vella. She's come to save Donner."

She gave a gasp and her eyes glistened with newly formed tears. I found myself enveloped in welcoming arms. I took great care to be cautious with her, her large pregnant belly a little awkward to hug around. Almost as awkward as it was for me to have a queen hug me so warmly. Healer or no, I was a simple girl from Vella. When

Torric had told me of the honor and respect I'd have in Glane, part of me had not quite believed him. And even though since I'd entered Glane no one had looked upon me with fear or disgust over being a healer, the warmth and acceptance of these brave people took me by surprise.

"Thank you," she said sincerely.

Nervously, I replied, "You're welcome. May I?" I reached my hand toward her rounded abdomen. When she nodded, I slipped my hand over the top of her belly and let that part of myself that I used for healing sink in. Inside, I could feel the vibrant spark of life. I grinned up at her. "The child will be very healthy."

"You can tell that?" she whispered in awe.

I nodded, and she turned her eyes to Torric, who was beaming at me. I blushed under his prideful gaze and turned away, but not before I noticed the question in her eyes. Too embarrassed to answer such things, I asked, "When can I meet Donner? I've journeyed long to do so."

She beckoned us into the apartments. I took a glance around; while the walls, floors, and ceilings were also in dark wood like Torric's room, in this room there were touches of a woman everywhere — from throw pillows, to lace atop tables. The hardwood floors had huge, intricately woven carpets of blue and green. The room itself was cheery and inviting. And as we made our way through the living area to the bedroom, I noticed the furniture design was in softer tones and lines.

When we entered the bedroom, there was a large canopy bed — and in its center, a man slept. He was tall, but thin, and his skin had a sickly pallor that contrasted deeply with his shock of dark auburn hair. Even without the sheen of sweat on his skin, I knew this was Donner as the need to heal him gripped me.

I started to approach the bed when Torric grabbed my hand and spun me around. "Are you sure you can do it?"

I smiled up at him and softly stroked his cheek. "Of course I can. I'll need to sleep a lot after."

Even though worry colored his eyes, he smiled. "I'll carry you back to our room after."

"*Our room?*" Sarine's voice rang with surprise.

"I'll tell you later," he grumbled.

I tuned them out and walked over to Donner. He was handsome in the classical sense, his features more refined than those of my ruggedly handsome warrior. I took his hand gently, and he slowly opened his eyes in confusion. His voice was barely a hoarse whisper. "Who…"

I let a soft smile take my face. "Shh. You rest now. When you wake up tomorrow, all will be well."

I knew if we had been a week later, it would have been too late. Taking his hand, I let my healing energies sink into him. I could feel it tracking down and burning the poison in his system. It did more than that, however, as I pushed myself to use more and sought to renew his strength.

When I was sure that the healing was complete, I released his hand and smiled. His gray eyes widened as he realized what I had done. Before I could faint, Torric's arms were around me. "Let's get you back."

In a meek little voice, I said, "I'll let you carry me."

He swept me up in his arms. I knew he was speaking, but I couldn't comprehend what he was saying as I felt the need to sleep press upon me. I drifted off before we even left the room. The soft brush of his lips fluttering across my temple was the last thing I felt before it went dark.

Chapter Twenty

A gentle hand stroked my hair as I felt consciousness slowly return. Before I even opened my eyes, I knew it was daylight. The hot sun was caressing my face, and I could see the pink of my eyelids.

I stretched languidly and then I smiled before I asked, "How's Donner?"

I heard a deep voice chuckle. "He's well now. Thanks to you."

Opening my eyes to meet Torric's impassioned emerald gaze, heat slowly started to build within me. For a long moment, our eyes remained locked. Leaning down, his lips caressed my mouth with a tender passion. I gasped softly, and his tongue swept into my mouth, delving in, stroking mine playfully. I slipped my hand into his hair and pulled him closer. His other hand started to meander over my body, and I felt flushed with desired that roared through my form.

My stomach growled. Torric sat up, laughing, and I blushed. This was not the time for a healer's need for food. I dragged the covers over my head as I felt him rise. Several moments later, I heard a plate being set on the nightstand. Sitting up, I found some bread and cheese waiting for me.

"I've ordered up some roast beef. Hopefully this will hold you over until then."

Nibbling on the food he gave me I asked, "How's Sarine?"

He grinned down at me. "Happy. And probably on her way here. I've no doubt the servant I sent for food is telling her you're awake."

My eyes went wide and I tossed the covers, about to rise. Pausing to take in my state, flames filled my cheeks. "You undressed me?"

He smiled wickedly as his eyes perused my body, eliciting a need within me once again. "Yes," he growled. "Sadly, that's all I did. You were in no condition to consent to anything more. Besides, I like you screaming my name, not snoring while I'm inside you."

Rolling my eyes, I slipped out of the bed and found my clothes draped across the back of the chair. I started to pull on my chemise when I felt Torric's hand run over my backside, around my waist, and up over my breasts. Once, I would have instantly blushed at such boldness; now, instead, desire flooded my veins with need. I gasped out, "What are you doing?"

He tugged softly at my nipples for a moment, drawing a sharp cry from me before he gently bit my neck and helped me pull down the chemise. His voice was husky in my ear. "Have I ever told you how well formed you are?"

"Well formed, huh?"

He nipped my ear. "Among other things."

"What other things?" I couldn't help preening a little at his words.

"Beautiful. Stunning. Sweet-tempered. And very warm."

Turning fully to him, I rose to my toes to give him a quick kiss before I turned to my dress. Checking myself in the mirror, I was glad that my hair was still in its braid from earlier. I tried to ignore the red in my cheeks. The plate by the bed beckoned, and I rushed over and began devouring the food. There was no sense in letting the queen see me gorging myself.

When we entered the main rooms, there was a knock on the door. Torric made his way over and opened it. First, Sarine glided into the room in a lovely emerald green silk gown that matched her eyes. She immediately beamed at me while I wished I were wearing a different color. She completely outshined me.

Donner, whom I almost didn't recognize, strode into the room behind her, his gray eyes seeking mine, alive with health. Life and warmth replaced the sickly pallor. His hair was now neatly arranged in short auburn curls. The leather pants and tunic were of the finest quality I had ever seen. It suddenly struck me that this was a king, and I had constantly referred to him as Donner as if I knew him. I snapped out of my musings and embarrassed, I curtsied. "Majesty."

In three quick strides, he was before me, and instantly he embraced me. His voice was heartfelt but higher in tone than Torric's. "You do not call me *majesty*. You've done me and my people a great service."

I giggled out of nerves and said. "Very well...Donner."

He smiled. "I didn't expect your hair to be so dark. From what I know, the best healers have flame-red hair."

"Oh, I dyed it for the last part of our journey. Give it half a week, and it'll be back to normal. Maybe less if I wash it fiercely enough."

He considered me, glanced at Torric, and then back. "Do you not want quarters of your own?"

"She stays with me," Torric said gruffly, his hard gaze locked on Donner.

The king's eyes lit up with mischief, and I knew in that instant that I liked him. He snickered. "Brother, she may not like your snoring."

Torric frowned. "I don't snore."

Delighted at the turnabout, I laughed. "Oh, yes, you do."

He pivoted to me with a surprised gleam in his gaze and I covered my mouth to hide my amusement. He shook his head, and then there was a knock on the door. Opening it, he found three servants with a cart overflowing with dishes containing food. They began setting the table for four. I shot Donner and Sarine a surprised look.

Sarine supplied, "We thought we could all eat together."

Torric peeked under the covered platters and frowned. "Bring some more food."

"Yes, my lord," a tall, thin servant girl said before she dashed off.

In surprise, Donner turned to Torric, who said, "After healing your sorry ass, she's going to need it."

Shock shot through me. But Donner just laughed good-naturedly. I studied him for a moment. He was nothing like how I would picture a king. But, then again, how many kings had I met before? Not one.

As we ate, Donner and Sarine asked me questions about my life in Vella. From their faces, I could see they were as upset as Torric had been about the way healers were treated. I wanted to ask them personal questions but felt shy about it. After all, they may have been nice, but they were still the rulers of Glane—and I was just a healer from a small village.

Once we finished eating, Donner asked me, "What are your plans?"

"My plans?"

He glanced over at Sarine before he said, "While we certainly hope you'll wish to stay here, we're wondering if you're planning on heading home to Vella."

I felt as if the three of them were holding their collective breath; even Torric was still worried about that. Healers now being so rare and valued in Glane, I was sure they would not want me to go. And I didn't want to go, either.

I smiled brightly before responding. "I would like to remain in Glane. However, I'd like to go back to Fort Nyte soon so I can resume training a girl there on how to be an herbalist. Perhaps after I finish training her, I could train others."

Donner smiled broadly. "That would be wonderful."

Sarine rose and said, "We should let them rest. It was a long journey here, and Zianya healed you so quickly after arriving."

Donner smiled lovingly at his wife. Rising, he rested his hand on her stomach a moment before sharing a tender look with her. My heart ached, and the fact that I'd healed this man moved me. This child would now know his or her father. Nodding to us, the two of them left. And I was instantly in Torric's arms.

Between his insistent kisses, he asked, "Where were we before your stomach so rudely interrupted us?"

I laughed as he hauled me off into the bedroom.

A few days later, I woke alone and stretched. Torric had warned me he'd be in a meeting with Donner this morning, so I wasn't very surprised.

Vonn had had dinner with us the night before and made his goodbyes. I was going to miss him and his gentle — if incessant — teasing. He had plans to go back to Fort Nyte to report to Keig, and then to go back to Pheon to spend several months with Meg. It was easy to convince Torric to stop by Pheon on our way back to Fort Nyte in order to see Vonn and Meg. I missed them both already.

Lying in the large bed, I wondered how I was going to spend the day. Torric hadn't told me when he'd be back, and I wasn't interested in lazing around his quarters all day. So I rose and went into the bathing chamber and took a too-long, hot bath before I got myself ready.

Looking in the mirror, I bit my bottom lip. I had been scrubbing my hair and washing it three times a day these last few days. It wasn't my bright flame red, but it was a nice dark red now. I let it fall freely, except for a braid across the crown of my head to keep it out of my eyes. Sarine had had some dresses altered for me. This one was a deep indigo, with pale blue crystals around a scoop neckline. It flowed in soft, velvet waves down the curves of my body.

Grinning with satisfaction, I left the room to wander the halls. It didn't take me long to become completely lost in the maze that made up Kingshold Castle. I paused at a window and noticed a beautiful garden full of early fall flowers. Deciding that was my destination, I started to stroll again. I made my way down the stairs, which was much easier than all the climbing.

It wasn't too long before I found myself turned around again. Finding a door that appeared to head outside, I opened it to find a huge library. I would have been excited if it wasn't for the fact that I couldn't read the written Glanean word. Regardless, I walked into the room. Pausing, I closed my eyes and smiled as the heavy scent of leather and paper surrounded me. Opening my eyes, I looked around at all of the many bookcases that went to the high ceilings. Wandering among them, I let my fingertips run over the leather-bound volumes of various colors.

Finding a staircase, I took it to the next level and discovered so many carefully arranged scrolls. I chose not to touch such ancient writings and after poking around a bit through the upstairs of the library and finding no other level, I went downstairs and headed out. I would have stayed longer, but not being able to read the words of even the titles made it unappealing to remain longer.

Colliding into someone, I gasped, "Oh, my apologies!"

"You should apologize," said a vaguely familiar voice that dripped with disdain.

I looked up to find Gemma staring at me if I were a mouse she found walking across her path. A smile crept across my lips. "Oh, hello, Gemma. How are you this fine day?"

Scowling, she replied, "Well enough…or I was until I came across something out of place."

I laughed, which just deepened her scowl. What she did not realize was that her scorn was not even close to that which I had often experienced back home in Vella. Senna would have sent Gemma off crying. My laugh turned her frown into a full-on sneer. I wanted to fold my arms, but instead, I placed my hands on my hips and tilted my head.

Her eyes turned to saucers before they narrowed as if I was some foul creature. "So are you Torric's latest toy?"

I felt the sting of those words, but I smiled instead. "Are you his old toy?"

Fury burned in her eyes. "I'm not his toy! Torric's never touched me."

I nodded. "Well, he's touched me. Repeatedly. I share his room, and he calls me his woman. I'm more than a toy. I'm certainly more than you."

She got right into my face. "He's mine. He's just waiting."

Calmly, I replied, "Waiting for what? Why don't you go find a man who actually wants you?"

She screeched, "He does want me!" Then she slapped me across the face. "You're just some peasant whore!"

"Gemma!" Sarine's hard voice cut through the girl's fury and her eyes were engulfed in chagrin. I stepped back and stared right at her as Sarine continued, "A healer is honored by all. Zianya used her gift to save our King, and this is how you treat her?"

"But she—"

"She what? Stated facts? Torric's tolerated your scheming because you're Donner's cousin, but I'll not allow you to call the woman who saved my husband a whore."

Gemma looked to Sarine and then to me. With her back to Sarine, her eyes belied her gentle words as she said, "I'm sorry to have insulted you, Zianya."

Brightly, I replied, "No offense taken. I wish you well."

She hurried off down the hall as Sarine came over to stand close to me. Once Gemma was well out of earshot, she said to me softly, "You were a bit harsh on her."

A groan escaped my lips as I dropped my hands. "I'm sorry. She hit a nerve, and I let myself react."

A soft affection flooded her face. "Well, she's wrong. I've never seen Torric so taken with a woman before. He's certainly never brought one here to share his room."

Embarrassment tore through me and I looked at her. "I kind of thought that might be the case."

"I've been meaning to comment on your pendant. It's quite striking. Is it a religious symbol?"

I laughed softly. "Well, don't tell Torric, but it is a protection symbol."

"Why not tell Torric?" Her eyes turned curious.

Beaming, I said, "He bought it for me on our trip here."

Her eyes enlarged in surprise. Within them was a question I didn't understand. For a moment, I thought she would give it voice, but then she shook her head.

I decided I couldn't take it anymore. "Why does everyone react so strangely when they find out Torric bought me a gift?"

She started down the hallway. "That isn't for me to—"

Frustration filled my voice as I finally begged, "Please. I don't understand, and I really want to."

She paused and turned to me. For a long moment, she searched my face and then rested her emerald eyes on the pendant once again. Finally, she said, "Before I say, can I ask you a personal question?"

I leaned against the wall and wrung my hands in front of my waist. "Of course."

"Were you and Torric first intimate before or after he gave you that pendant?"

I giggled nervously, a habit I could never seem to break, and looked away. I hadn't expected that question. I wasn't sure how to react other than the intense heat on my cheeks.

"I know it's very personal, but it's important."

"Well, it was after," I stated shyly.

She pursed her lips as she thought about it. Finally, she asked, "He didn't tell you what that means?"

"No. Please tell me?"

"When a warrior courts the woman he thinks is his True Mate, he gives her a pendant. He's careful not to make love to her before he gives that to her. When she's ready to accept being his True Mate, they make love for the first time. It's a very old tradition. But you're not from Glane, and you don't know what this means. I don't know what it means either, because of that reason. I would have thought Torric would have explained it to you." For several long moments, she stared at my pendant, contemplating.

"So…you don't have marriages?" I found the whole thing confusing. My parents had been True Mates, but according to my mother, they hadn't been intimate until after they were married.

However, she could have been lying about it so that I would wait for marriage.

She sighed. "We do. But if you're True Mates, the bond is considered just as binding."

I frowned. "But he didn't tell me."

"Like I said, I don't know what this means."

She looked as confused as I felt. Taking a deep breath, I nodded. Meeting her eyes, I smiled and asked, "Can you direct me to that lovely garden outside?"

Once outside, I took the time to wander the area. It was large and protected by three walls, the fourth being the castle itself. There were several large cherry and apple trees that were heavy with fruit that wasn't quite ripe. Wandering deeper, I found a swing and sat down. Gently, I swayed back and forth as I contemplated what Sarine had said. Either Torric didn't mean to take me as his True Mate or, for reasons I didn't understand, he had chosen not to explain it to me. I just didn't know how to process this information.

"Want me to push?"

I turned to find Torric standing there, staring at me in such a way that caused heat to flood my veins. But when I thought about what Sarine had said, cold shot through me as annoyance flashed through my heart. He arched an eyebrow in confusion.

It took but a moment for me to grab my pendant and hold it up. "Care to explain this to me?"

His face fell. "Who told you?"

"That's not as important as why you didn't."

He strode over to me and paused before me. Slipping his hands over my cheeks, he leaned down so we were eye to eye. Even though I knew that I should not, I couldn't help but pout. I felt betrayed. This was something he should have told me right from the beginning.

He kissed my brow. "I was going to tell you."

"When?"

He let out a frustrated groan and ran his hand through his hair. "I was planning on telling you before we were together the first time. But then, after I saw you there on that stake, I went a little crazy about how I nearly lost you, and I lost control. I needed you to reassure myself that you were alive and in my arms. And your eyes when you looked at me were so trusting and willing. How could I resist you?"

"So you think I'm your True Mate? How?"

He softly stroked my hair back. "When I first saw you asleep in your home, I didn't really know what it was. I just knew I needed you, that you were not like any other woman I had ever seen. But I had to bring you to Donner. I knew I couldn't take advantage of you like that. But each day I was with you, listening to you talk, smelling your sweet scent, I found myself lost. When we were in that market, just before we left, I just suddenly knew. That's why I had to get you something. I was intent on telling you. But when I came back, those men were trying to drag you away, and I nearly lost it. It wasn't the right time."

My mind whirled back through our journey together. "But when you gave me the pendant, why didn't you tell me?"

He sighed and pulled me up and into his arms. His lips played softly against my ear with a few kisses before he said, "When the time finally came, I thought you'd know what it meant, but you didn't. I wasn't sure how you'd react if I told you, but I needed you to have it. I knew that once we got into Glane and men realized I had given it to you, none of them would touch you. Maybe it was a bit selfish, but the idea of another man lying with you drove me insane. I figured I'd court you and ask you later."

I smiled and curled up into his arms.

He held me tighter. "I know I should've told you before we were together that first night. I'm sorry I didn't, but I'm not sorry that I was finally able to have you as I needed. I'm hoping we'll continue to be together. I know that things are different in Renth, but…"

I stared up at him, fear ran through me. But after everything he just said, I had to be courageous. "Does this mean…you love me?"

He lifted an eyebrow. "Do you have to ask?"

I blushed and turned away. When my eyes returned to him, he frowned. So I said, "I'm just nervous about your feelings. Things like this aren't easy for me. I mean, if you don't love me—"

"Of course I love you," he said, his voice rough with emotion. "I'm just not one to usually say such things."

I grinned up at him. "Well, maybe you could try to say it once in a while, and I'll try to live with you not saying it all the time. Because I've loved you for a while now, and I've been too afraid to tell you."

He tugged me closer and roughly placed his lips on mine. His heat seeped into my body, fusing me to him. All this time, fear had kept me from sharing what I felt, and it was all for nothing. If I had just been a little more perceptive, I would have noticed his love in every touch, in every kiss. I opened my mouth to him and he delved hungrily into it with his tongue.

Leading me deeper into the wooded area of the garden, he leaned back against a tree and grinned at me. His intent clear, I gasped out, "Someone will see!"

"Once, long ago, people wandered this garden. Not anymore. The only reason I knew you were here is that Sarine told me I should go see you in the garden. Trust me."

I laughed. "Trust you? You mean the man who just wants under my skirt."

His teeth gently grazed beneath my ear. "No—the man who loves you."

I went weak in the knees as his mouth ran over my neck, nipping here and there, igniting a fire in me. His hands stroked over me, causing my body to quake in his arms. When his lips returned to mine, I opened my mouth and returned his kiss with a desperate passion. Boldly, I let my hand slip between us and worked on the ties of his leather pants. He pulled back, his heated eyes watching me as my fingers flew over the ties to free him.

Yanking my skirt up, he slipped his hands over my bottom and lifted me. Then we were one, and he moved against me in slow, powerful thrusts as he held me tight. Fire roared through my veins, and I cried out his name. He bit my bottom lip and sucked softly, looking into my eyes, his gaze urging me to new heights. My body coiled and tensed around him and then, suddenly, I was quaking wildly in his arms as he growled and picked up speed. His name fervently tore from my lips over and over as I built to a second peak. When at last our release took us, the intensity left me breathless as he sank down to lean against the tree, holding me to him, keeping us one, as he breathed heavily and growled, "Never doubt me again."

Just as breathless, I whimpered. "I won't."

Roughly, he gripped my hips to him. "And I'll give you a proper wedding. I know you people of Renth find such things important."

I grinned up at him. "Well, I used to be of Renth, but I'm a citizen of Glane now."

He squeezed me tightly to him. "My woman."

Nipping his neck, I said, "Yours."

Chapter Twenty-One

Four days later, Donner decided to have a formal introduction of the Healer of Glane to the current court. My nervous heart fluttered like a small bird until I thought it would fly away. I didn't want to be the center of attention. My happiness was in just healing those whom I came across in need. To me, this was unnecessary.

There was another reason I was worried, however. Donner's poisoning occurred during an attack, but there had been no cut. I had decided that it was probably some sort of assassin that had done it. If that assassin was still around, would he then come after me? I knew that Torric would do whatever was necessary to protect me, but what if it wasn't enough? What if they still killed me? The idea of my death had never been something that frightened me. Until now. Now, the idea of being dead and leaving Torric's side shook me to the core.

And then there was the other reason Donner had to introduce me to the court. Sarine decided that Torric would announce that I was his True Mate and that we were going to have a formal wedding. I had no doubt Gemma would be furious, but I didn't really care about her feelings. I wanted to marry Torric. In Renth, only an actual wedding ceremony had any legitimacy. What I wasn't sure of was the idea of a large, formal wedding. When Sarine had heard about our decision, she had been so excited she suggested the formal court wedding. How could I deny Torric's sister? Even if she wasn't the queen, I wouldn't have been able to say no.

Silently, I followed Torric into the throne room. Upon a large dais, Donner lounged on a large, white marble throne, the tall back of which reminded me of a trio of spearheads. Sarine sat at his side on a demure throne of white marble that was as graceful and elegant as she was. We walked down the aisle, the small assemblage of lords and ladies watching us and studying my flame-red hair curiously. We took stance near Sarine's side of the dais.

Glancing across to Donner's side, I found Gemma looking at me with wide, hateful eyes. I schooled my expression into a neutral one and met her gaze. Torric's large, warm hand took mine, and her eyes nearly fell out of their sockets. Turning from her, I glanced up at Donner. He gave me a quick wink. Calm immediately flooded through my body. My place was in Glane now, by Torric's side. All of this was just a formality. I could handle formality. Couldn't I?

I let out a soft, shuddery breath as my blood ran cold. It was like a twitch in the back of my mind. I felt eyes upon me, and I didn't think they were Gemma's.

Turning my head slightly, I let my gaze search the large hall. It paused on a man with ink-black curls and eyes so dark, they, too, seemed black. He was handsome, in a roguish sort of way, with neatly trimmed facial hair. Yet his icy dark gaze sent a shiver of fear through me. Quickly, I turned my gaze back to Donner. He was rising.

"Lords and Ladies. I come before you a new man. The poison, which has plagued me in recent months, has left my system. We owe our gratitude to a daughter of Glane who has returned to us from Renth. Zianya, Healer of Vella, is descended of one of the healers of our own land who escaped the treachery that happened so long ago. With her return, we hope that the tides of this war will change, that healers will once again grace our lands. With that in mind, I name Zianya the Healer of Glane, and look forward to the skills she can teach our people."

Deep, hot red took my cheeks as loud clapping sounded around the room. Glancing around, I noted that Gemma was politely clapping. The man with the ink-black curls also joined in the applause, but his eyes continued to burn into me. I wondered if Torric noticed. When I turned my eyes up to him, I found him looking to Donner, waiting for his word. "Before our feast, Torric, Duke of Northold, wishes to speak."

In an instant, Torric swept me up onto the dais to face everyone. I thought I had been embarrassed during Donner's formal proclamation, but as Torric swept me up there, my heart hammered in fear and discomfiture. I hadn't known he was going to have me face everyone. Chewing on my lower lip, I stared at the back of the room, too afraid to meet anyone's eye. But even while doing this, I could feel the eyes of the court on me. They all were wondering what it was I was doing there. I swallowed and forced myself to glance around the room. Gemma looked livid.

Torric's rich voice boomed out, "I will keep this brief. As you all know, I don't care for courtly matters. In Zianya, I have found my True Mate. As is the custom of the people of Renth, we will also have a marriage ceremony in one month. That is all."

For a moment, there was stunned silence. Then the lords and ladies of the court burst into applause. As my eyes ran over the room, I noticed Gemma simply staring at me in utter amazement. A twinge of guilt stabbed at my heart. The poor girl had probably thought that when Torric discarded me, she would be his wife. Regret over my harsh words to her filled me. Before I could let it consume me, I let my gaze wander again and found the dark-haired man staring at me with calculation in his eyes. I wondered who he was. But before I could quietly ask, Torric hurried me out of the room to the court dining room.

Later, when we were alone in our room, he asked, "Well?"

I laughed. "Can we not just run off and have a small ceremony? Just the two of us?"

Amusement twinkled in his emerald eyes. "Do you want to tell my sister?"

I frowned. "No. She'd never forgive me."

There was a knock at the door. Torric opened it to reveal Sarine. She slipped into the room and pulled me into her arms. "My dear, you looked so frightened in there. Sorry for the spectacle."

I smiled weakly. "It isn't in my nature to be the center of attention."

"Well, sadly, you'll have to learn to accept it. Donner is just finishing up with the court. After that, how about the four of us have a small meal? I noticed that just like Donner and I, you hardly touched a thing at that stuffy feast. Also, we can start planning." She squealed the last sentence, and that brought a smile to my lips.

Torric was right—how could I tell Sarine that I didn't want a formal wedding? Instead, I nodded in agreement. "That sounds like a wonderful idea."

"A red dress is traditional here in Glane, but would you rather have a traditional Renth style?"

"Pale blue is traditional in Renth." I pursed my lips and thought about it for a moment. "However, I'm from Glane now. So red it is."

Torric made himself scarce as the two of us talked about various traditions for weddings that either Glane or Renth had. As we did, Sarine decided it would be appropriate to mix some of Renth's traditions with Glane's. I honestly did not care that much; I was already Torric's, and he was mine. That was all that really mattered to me in the end.

When Donner joined us, we called for a light meal. As Torric and Donner spoke of strategy, Sarine told me that I would be going to her dressmaker. Considering the lovely dresses the queen always wore, I felt safe in her dressmaker's hands.

"Just not too ostentatious. All of this is rather new to me. I've always tried to have people ignore me because I'm not one for confrontation."

Sarine laughed. "You could have fooled me. Gemma will never be the same."

I smiled. "Well, I don't like confrontation, but I'm not one to shrink from a challenge, either. I had a delicate line to walk back home, but I think not living in fear loosened my tongue."

She let out an angry huff. "The fools. They had a healer in their midst. They should have revered you."

Nervous laughter bubbled forth. "I'm not sure I want to be revered, either. I just want to live a simple life, with Torric."

His arm was suddenly around me, dragging my chair closer to his. When I looked up, I found him smiling down at me. "That's all I want, too."

Donner quipped, "Being the Duke and Duchess of Northold, your lives won't be that simple."

I groaned. "Can't I be Torric's wife without being a duchess?"

Torric frowned at me. "You don't want my title?"

Smiling up at him, I replied, "You know that I don't care about such things, I've never loved you for your title."

Kissing my brow, he held me close for one quiet moment. "I know. It's one of the many things I love about you. But you need the title. Otherwise there will be women who will think they can come between us."

The thought of Gemma trying to seduce Torric rushed through my jealous mind. I frowned. "Duchess it is."

Donner laughed. "Don't be so enthusiastic, oh Healer of Glane."

At that moment, there was a burst through the door. The man with the ink-black curls charged in. He looked surprised to see Donner and Sarine. Then his eyes locked on me with hatred, and I shrank back. Torric jumped up and pushed me behind him.

"Donner, guard the women!" With that, he attacked the assassin—for that could only be what he was.

Grabbing Sarine and me, Donner pulled us back to the far wall. He grabbed one of Torric's blades from his small weapons workbench. My eyes locked onto Torric. He had just a small, formal dagger that he'd worn to court. The two struggled around the room. I thought there was no one who could be a match for my warrior, but this man was quick and strong. Every time it seemed that Torric had the upper hand, the man would whirl from his grasp and attack from a different angle. But I had faith that my Torric would win.

And then, like a blade through my heart, I felt it. The desire to heal combined with the need to not touch. He stumbled back and my eyes went wide. My Torric was dying. And, Spirits help me, I couldn't let that happen. Not when I knew there was one thing I could do, no matter how forbidden it was.

I dashed over to the assassin, Sarine crying out my name in shock and fear. With a grim gaze, I grasped the assassin's arm. Instead of permitting my healing energy to flow into him, I drew life from him. He turned his black eyes over at me and raised his blade. I held strong as his eyes went wide and he became too weak to hold his own weapon. He tried to pull away, but in his rapidly weakening state, he could barely move. Sinking to his knees, he stared up at me in abject terror as the truth of what was happening sank into his mind.

It was then that I allowed myself to remember when my mother had given me a pet rabbit. At the time, I was only ten. She had told me to take great care of it, and I named it Bun-Bun. I loved that fluffy, gray rabbit and spent a lot of time caring for it. Then one day, my mother told me to touch the rabbit and reverse the flow of my healing. I refused. She once again demanded that I hold onto Bun-Bun and drain him of his life. I didn't want to do it, but she would not relent until I did. As the last of his little life ebbed away, tears tore through me. My mother had said, "Remember the pain of this loss. This is why we forbid this particular art. As a healer, we never want to use our powers this way. So remember this pain as a reason why you never do this."

I had sworn I would never drain anyone or anything again. Yet here I was, draining the last of this assassin's life as he slumped onto the floor. His nearly black eyes were gaping up at me in horror. I could see the realization that was in those eyes slowly fading away as they glassed over. He was dying. Yet the pain I felt in killing this way did not compare to the agony I felt at the thought of Torric dying. We had not come this far just to let one assassin take him from me.

When the assassin died, I felt so amazingly full of power. It was in that moment, as a trained adult, that I finally realized why healers forbid such use of power. The power within me was magnificent! It was intoxicating! If I drained people, I could heal myself. I could probably live forever off the life energy of others. But that was not what I wanted.

"Torric!" Sarine screamed. There wasn't much time left.

Going to Torric's side, I pushed the healing energy, the energy that I stole, into him. As strength flowed into him, I removed the knife from his chest. For a moment, it bled and then stitched up quickly as I knitted his wound together and burned the poison that had been on the blade out of his body. He turned his eyes to me, astonishment filled his gaze, and he touched my cheek with a sense of wonder. He was well. Fully healed. And then, I let the sleep take me.

"She's coming around." Sarine's voice was quiet, reverent.

My mind was foggy. I rolled onto my side and curled up to my pillow with a moan. A gentle hand stroked my hair, and I smiled as I recognized the gentle touch of rough fingers. "Wake up, my little healer."

Slowly, I opened my eyes to find Torric leaning down and looking at me, awe filling his glorious emerald gaze. I smiled and reached for him. Then the realization hit me, and I sat up quickly, swaying a moment with a hand to my head before I grabbed him. "Torric! Are you all right?"

He frowned. "Am I all right? Zianya, what did you do?"

My eyes sought out Donner's. I was surprised to see his gaze as confused as everyone else's. Perhaps because his healing powers were not strong enough, he didn't know. Perhaps because of this, no one had thought to tell him. Chewing my bottom lip, I looked down at my hands, which were twisting. Shyly, I raised my eyes to Torric's and said, "I did something bad."

"Bad?" Donner blurted out, "Spirits above, woman, you were amazing! You killed Crede and saved Torric."

"You knew him?"

Sarine's eyes darkened as she spoke. "We thought we did. But now that I'm thinking about it, it wasn't long after Crede came to court that the raid occurred and Donner was poisoned."

"Who was he?"

"Crede from Allwen," Donner explained. "He recently inherited from his father. Although, it has been a long time since I saw Bolton. It had been years since a lord from Allwen had been to court. Perhaps I should dispatch a small force to see what's going on there."

Torric nodded, but his eyes remained locked on me. "How did you do that?" he asked quietly.

Exhaling softly, I replied, "I told you there were secrets healers had. It's a forbidden thing. When I was very young, my mother forbid me from using it. But…well, I knew that it could save you, so I just didn't care if I did such a forbidden thing. Killing the man who was trying to take you from me didn't matter. You mattered."

Sitting on the bed, he drew me into his warm embrace. Gently, in my ear, he whispered, "Thank you for saving my life."

I heard the door quietly click as Donner and Sarine left. Turning my eyes to Torric's, I leaned over and kissed him. He pressed me to him and deepened the kiss. Passion and desperation churned into a heady mixture that left me breathless.

He pushed me onto my back, and his hands ran over my breasts. I trembled in need, and suddenly all of the clothing I had on felt as if it were suffocating me. I reached for the ties on the back of my dress when suddenly my stomach grumbled. Loudly.

That was really starting to annoy me.

However, Torric just laughed into my neck and rained soft kisses and licks on my collarbone. "We'll continue this after I feed you. Come on, I think the food we ordered earlier is still on the table."

"It's still here? How long was I asleep?"

"Only an hour."

"Must be because…" My stomach made an insistent noise that had me blushing and Torric laughing as he scooped me up.

As we headed into the next room, I realized that a state wedding was a small sacrifice to have the love of this man forever. I vowed not to complain when the planning started in earnest.

But for now, I only had one plan. That was to make passionate love to my warrior. Once I filled my belly, of course.

Epilogue

Fourteen months later found me riding before Torric as we left Fort Nyte. I wish I could say the war magically ended when they discovered Glane had a healer again, but that was not the case. If anything, Moritzan had stepped up its offensive. Because of this, I had a job to do—the first of many such jobs having just been completed.

I had spent a better part of a year training Kayla to be an herbalist and to work with the medics in the healing hall. While I'd been away, she had made a study of all our notes a priority. When I returned, she devoured the information I gave her. I had always been a healer first and an herbalist second. But her singular devotion to the craft had transformed her, and I knew it would not be long before she exceeded me in the knowledge of herbs.

Another surprise when I had returned was that she was in a relationship. With Zeer. He was as quiet as always, but she lit up like a star whenever she saw him. Ten days before Torric and I left Fort Nyte, the two of them had married. Their wedding had been a simple affair, something I would have preferred to the pompous state occasion Torric and I had endured. But I couldn't really complain because Sarine was right—state weddings gave the people hope. She told me my next task was to have a baby. Torric and I were working on that with great enthusiasm. Being a healer meant it would probably take a long time…but I certainly didn't mind the work.

As we started to set up camp for the evening, I found Torric's eyes upon me with a look that set my soul ablaze. I grinned and started to make a stew over the fire. He still didn't like me cooking when we were out like this, but I didn't care. I worked cautiously, so his worry about me burning myself was misplaced. I also finally learned to cook meat properly over an open flame.

Journeying alone together like this reminded me of when we first met. I had been so very frightened to discover a large and powerful warrior had kidnapped me. Now, I would not change one thing. I knew that I would have been too scared to agree to go to Glane with him. His taking me was the only way. His taking me had opened my world.

After we ate and cleaned the campsite, he dragged me into the tent. His desire burned in his eyes and caused a tremor through my body. He ran his hands over me, his emerald gaze not leaving mine. Our hands flew rapidly over each other's clothing, leaving me breathless and wanting. As we joined into one, his lips were on mine, and I knew that I would never be that lonely woman on the mountain again. I was complete now. I was home.

I hope you enjoyed The Healer and the Warrior. If you did, I would **greatly appreciate** *it if you'd take just a couple of moments to write a short review on Amazon. Doing so helps others to find my books, but it also helps me get to know what my readers think. Thank you in advance!*

Interested in discovering my other work? Check it out here:

https://www.amazon.com/Bekah-Clark/e/B00XUQ4YUS?ref_=pe_1724030_132998060

Want to connect with me? Interested in my lookbook? You can find me on the following:

http://www.bekahclarkbooks.com/

https://twitter.com/BekahClarkBooks

https://www.facebook.com/BekahClarkBooks/

https://www.pinterest.com/bekahclarkbooks/

Books by Bekah Clark

Rise of the Hawk series:
The Hawk in Winter
The Raven in Spring
The Peacock in Summer
The Vulture in Fall
(The Complete Series is also available in one book)

The Empress and the Assassin

The Healer and the Warrior series:

The Healer and the Warrior
(Untitled #2) Summer 2018

The Stone Sisters series:

The Stone Sisters: Lyssa
The Stone Sisters: Lexa (2018)
The Stone Sisters: Untitled (2019)

The Frozen Queen series:

The Frozen Queen: Reluctant Heir
The Frozen Queen: Suspended Heart (2018)
The Frozen Queen: Renewed (2019)

Made in United States
Troutdale, OR
09/15/2023

12919721R00131